THE CHOSEN ONES

DIA LYNNE CARDO

STRATTON
—PRESS—
Publishing Life

THE CHOSEN ONES
Copyright © 2019 **Dia Lynne Cardo**

All rights reserved. No part of this book may be used or reproduced by any means, graphic, electronic, or mechanical, including photocopying, recording, taping or by information storage and retrieval system without the written permission of the author except in the case of brief quotations embodied in critical articles and reviews.

Stratton Press, LLC
1603 Capitol Ave, Suite 310,
Cheyenne, WY 82001
www.stratton-press.com
1-888-323-7009

Because of the dynamic nature of the Internet, any web addresses or links contained in this book may have changed since publication and may no longer be valid. The views expressed in the work are solely those of the author and do not necessarily reflect the views of the publisher, and the publisher hereby disclaims any responsibility for them.

ISBN (Paperback): 978-1-64345-293-7
ISBN (Ebook): 978-1-64345-386-6

Printed in the United States of America

We become what we wish to become
in the end.

—Unknown

COYOTE HUNTER
(SHE WHO DARES)

Endurance and faith must be within every man
who conquers this appalling world.
—Unknown

Chapter One

Coyote Hunter was trotting and panting with her labor pains as she crossed the prairie in the hot Texas sun. She knew her babe was coming soon. She had strayed too far from the hut in her search for meat.

Her hunt was successful. She was an experienced tracker and had found a den of coyotes. The results hung from her hunting belt. There would be meat to eat while she recuperated from the imminent birth of her babe. She had to make it back to the hut before the babe was born. She did not wish to become meat for hungry wild animals when she was in her weakest moments of childbirth.

Another tearing labor pain reminded her that this babe was inpatient to be born; she trotted at a faster pace.

It felt to her as if a lengthy time passed before she reached the one-room hut where she lived. The hut provided only basic shelter. It was weak, very much like her husband's character. She thought with relief, *At least I will have shade from the overpowering, hot Texas sun.*

Coyote Hunter's husband was in the fields scraping the hard Texas soil. She did not call for him as she labored. She knew he would be of no use. She did not need him. She hurriedly made her preparations to give birth. There wasn't enough time; she was panting through each contraction. She felt an agonizing pain rip through her abdomen. She accepted it joyfully and thought, *Good, the birth pains are coming closer and harder. It is nearly time to meet the new babe.* She was Apache. Her husband would never take that away from her. She thought with a flash of anger, *I may have been forced to marry this vicious white man, but I am not required to adopt his ways.*

She squatted on the floor of the hut. She chanted to the Great Spirit for the birth of a strong son to satisfy her husband. As she chanted, her memories brought back all the reasons she was here with this white man. She had been given to her husband in an Apache trade deal. She left her tribe for the bride price of twenty wild horses. These horses would feed her starving tribe for many moons.

Her husband brought about this handsome offer to the Great Chief soon after he watched her bathe in the communal pond. The Great Chief saw that it would give her much honor among her people and had accepted the white man's offer. The Great Chief could not imagine what her life would be like with this white man. Coyote Hunter was sure that the Great Chief would have rejected his offer if he had known the treatment Coyote Hunter would endure. The Apaches did not mistreat their women; they were treasured and a prideful asset to their Braves.

She could not understand why her husband traded for her. It was obvious he was unhappy with his end of the bargain. She asked her spirit many times, "Why would he pay such a high bride price for me if he intended only to abuse me? Surely all white men are not the same. If they are, then my heart grieves for all of my sisters who have met the same fate."

An Apache man would have held her close to his heart; he would have shown a deep pride, unique only to him, in owning her. Her beauty was great. She had long raven hair to her waist that glistened with midnight blue highlights. Her eyes were large, thick-lashed, and bit with a glistening deep warning black when angry. She was still slender in spite of her pregnancy. She believed her husband did not see her as beautiful. He desired her, he desired to own her, yet he did not love her. She could not love him. His abuse made her guard her heart, distrust him, and wait for his next rage that would bring his fist to her face. She was not afraid of him. Apaches did not show their fear or their pain.

Coyote Hunter believed she was worthy of something better than her husband. And then she realized that these thoughts were not praiseworthy. All Apaches know not to question the Great Spirit's ways. Coyote Hunter must believe she had been honored. She had been used by the Great Spirit to save her people from starvation. Her husband, Mitch, had been used as well. She must respect him.

She reached down between her legs. She loosened the babe's shoulder from her vaginal canal. It was nearly time for the birth. She could see the babe's hair color now, raven like her own. She was joyous; it was not blond like her husband's. She prayed from her heart that the babe did not have the white man's light eyes.

She felt a strong urge to push down, but she cautioned herself to be patient and allow her body to bring forth the babe naturally. She would find out the sex of the babe soon.

After another gripping pain, she felt the pain of the babe sliding through her birth canal. She suffered through an intense ripping sensation the length of her birth canal. Happiness flooded through her. The Apache believed this ripping was a sign of a lucky birth. Her babe would not be born dead. She would have a large healthy baby. She had hoped for this.

She had made the necessary preparations. She had gathered the absorbable lint that grew wild on the prairie for packing wounds. This lint would stop the bleeding and allow healing. She had followed the old ways in all of her preparations for this birth. These ways had been taught to her by the elderly Apache women. She took into her heart every word they spoke.

She had prepared everything the babe would need, most of them by using the coyote skins from her hunts. She made all of the clothes, blankets, loincloths, and a special carrying sling for the babe.

Coyote Hunter made no sound as the babe slid the rest of the way out of her birth canal. She saw that she was mother to a daughter. The babe had sharp black eyes and did not cry. Coyote Hunter examined her babe and felt a surge of protectiveness enter into her heart and soul. She thought, *This babe is strong. She will make a fine hunter.* Coyote Hunter placed her in a sling that held the babe next to her breast and left her own arms free. The babe nuzzled and began to nurse.

The babe was born on an auspicious day for the Apaches. It was the day the prairie flowers opened their purple blossoms to reach for the early morning gentle rays of sunlight. Coyote Hunter decided to call the babe Prairie Blossom until she earned her spirit name. It was the Apache way.

Coyote Hunter was only ten years old when she earned her spirit name. Her gift for running was made evident by the Great Spirit when he allowed her to outrun her first coyote, butcher it, and bring it back to her starving tribe. The Medicine Man renamed her Coyote Hunter and gave her the right to hunt with spear and knife. There was a powerful ceremony. His chanting was loud as he prayed to the spirits. It was important that they hear and know her as a female hunter in the great beyond.

Coyote Hunter's memories captivated her heart. She desired to return to her people. She rationalized that Prairie Blossom must be introduced to the Spirit World. Coyote Hunter would take her to the Apache tribe before anything could happen to her. She must be known by the spirits should something befall her and take her life. It was the responsibility belonging to Coyote Hunter, not her white husband.

Her excitement grew to momentous proportions. She thought, *There would be much joy and feasting to celebrate the birth of the babe. The Medicine Man would chant, and he would pass his holy fragrant smoke across the babe. He would name the babe Prairie Blossom.* She would ask the Medicine Man to chant to the spirits for a powerful spirit name and the power to defeat her enemy when the time came.

Coyote Hunter felt that she was only beseeching the spirits for what was destined to happen in the babe's future. She would have a name even more powerful than her mother's name. It was evident that she was born with knowledge. It was apparent in her eyes—they were keen, sharp, and intuitive.

Coyote Hunter began to make her plans. She would leave for the ceremony at dawn. It was a two-day trot for Coyote Hunter. She wanted to see her people and for them to see Prairie Blossom. Oh, Coyote Hunter missed them. She could scarcely wait for dawn to break.

She awoke early and sprinted out of the hut seeing dawn's golden light coated with a pale violet mist throughout the vast Texas sky. She spoke to herself, "I must wake Prairie Blossom and nurse her. Then, I must leave. If the Great Spirit allows, I will run with the wind spirits to the loving bosom of my people."

Coyote Hunter prayed, "Oh, Great Spirit, please allow your servant to reach her loved ones. Please guide and protect this weak woman. Please let the babe be introduced to the Spirit World. I have placed all my trust in you, Great Spirit."

THE CHOSEN ONES

The Great Spirit intended to answer her prayer, but not as Coyote Hunter trusted within her heart. There would be much for her to endure, and she would not understand the Great Spirit's purposes. Her heart would believe the Great Spirit had abandoned her. He had not. He used Coyote Hunter to make a way for his future chosen ones. All Apache know the Great Spirit blesses those he uses.

Chapter Two

Coyote Hunter's husband retuned from the fields at evening's light. He was filthy and angry due to the stubbornness of the western Texas soil. Prairie Flower was strapped in her sling next to Coyote Hunter's breast. Coyote Hunter was cooking for her husband. Mostly it was tortillas and beans; he could provide no more than that. Coyote Hunter provided for herself. He did not know that she ate well every day. Her chief allowed her to keep this secret from her husband lest he attempt to use it for his own gain.

Her husband was not aware that her spirit name was literal in its meaning. He did not wish to learn her ways, and she felt no guilt. She thought, *He is weak and is not deserving of meat.*

The Apache cared only for the very young and the very old. These ones were not hunters and must be provided for. Each Brave provided for his women and offspring.

Coyote Hunter had never provided her husband with meat. It was not her duty. He was an unworthy, pitiful creature in her eyes.

Mitch saw the sling wrapped over Coyote Hunter's shoulder. He said, "So, the brat has come. What is it anyway? I warn you, squaw. It had better be a son to grow and help me scratch a living out of my cruel land."

Coyote Hunter calmly replied, "It is a girl child, husband. A very beautiful girl child." Mitch flew into one of his rages. He stalked Coyote Hunter into a corner of the hut. She was not afraid; she only wished to protect Prairie Blossom. She tightened her hands instinctively on the babe as she backed away from her husband. He was unaware, but she was prepared to kill him if he attempted to hurt the babe. The sling she had made concealed her butchering knives. She could grasp one at the same moment that he should decide to harm the babe.

He balled up his fist and punched Coyote Hunter in the nose. Blood splattered. She made not a sound or a movement, but her eyes were red with rage and hate. The babe began to cry as if she felt her mother's pain.

Mitch screamed at Coyote Hunter, "Can't you do anything right? I need sons, not another mouth to feed. Now, I am saddled with a useless brat. If you weren't lately out of childbed, I would beat you black and blue. You are a useless Indian squaw. See this fist?" He shook it angrily in Coyote Hunter's face. "I will beat you soon, and I will beat you hard. Look forward to your beating. I will not forget your lack of providing me with a strong son. You shut that brat up, do you hear me?" He seized his tortillas and left the hut.

Coyote Hunter calmed the babe with her breast and soft croons as if to say, "All is fine now, little one."

Once the babe was calm, she cleaned the blood off herself and off the new sling. She was not surprised by her husband's reaction to a girl child; she had known that he would hit her. She did not fear his beatings. He was only a weak man. He had no good qualities. She had no respect for his threats or beatings. She also knew that he could not hurt her if she did not allow him to. She was an Apache; she endured his abuse without a sound. Her only grief was that he knew so little. He did not know the value and honor a well-treated woman could bring to him.

Coyote Hunter soon became strong-minded by her hate-filled thoughts. She decided that her husband would never lay a hand on Prairie Blossom. She would never have to endure a cruel and hateful father. Coyote Hunter would kill him if he ever touched the babe in rage or even in affection. She imagined what she would do. She spoke a vow to the Great Spirit. She would strip off his skin piece by piece and leave him for the wild animals to finish if he ever touched the babe. Prairie Blossom would never feel his fist or his attempts for her affection. She felt her husband was of no worth and would have no respect from the babe or herself. She was sure the Great Spirit did not expect her to respect this puny white man and his abusive ways.

After this decision, Coyote Hunter calmly began to make her plans for her trip to the Apache tribal lands. She would tell her husband before she left with the dawn. She would also dare him to touch Prairie Blossom. He would see the hate in her eyes, true Apache hate reserved only for their worst enemies. He would see that she would only warn him once. He was a coward. He would run from that kind of heartfelt hate. He would know that her hate for him would mean the end of his life if he disobeyed.

The Great Spirit had given her very special gifts. She could run like the wind, she could kill, and she could butcher her kill. If he ever touched Prairie Blossom, he would only be one more kill. She would see that he understood.

Chapter Three

Coyote Hunter rose earlier than usual the next morning. She used the time to pack all she and the babe would need. She nursed the babe and laid Prairie Blossom amid the things she had packed. She thought she would be safe there; you could not see her. She brewed coffee in hopes the odor would wake her husband. She sat patiently and waited for her husband to open his eyes. She watched him while he slept and nurtured the hate in her heart.

Her vigilance was rewarded. He rolled over and saw her staring at him. Hate and menace was glinting from her eyes.

He started violently. He bellowed, "What are you looking at, squaw?"

She knew he sought to intimidate her, but she would not allow him to gain the advantage. She said, "I am looking at a pitifully weak man, my husband."

He began to move from the bed. No doubt, he intended to beat her.

She stopped him with a warning glare. He became very still, as if he had seen a coiled rattler in the hut.

She said, "I am going to the Apache tribal lands. I am going to have the Holy Ceremony performed over Prairie Blossom. I will be among my people. I will be back in two turns of the moon. Prairie Blossom must be introduced to the spirits so they will know her in the Great Beyond. It is our way with all newborns and our duty to them. I have said the last pleasant words that I will say to you. However, I have unpleasant words to say to you. I warn you now, you will never lay a hand on Prairie Blossom. If you do this, I will kill you. I have made this vow to the Great Spirit." Her eyes were flashing with an inward light; they were full of malevolence. In combination with the mottled face he had given her the night before, they were utterly Apache.

Her husband said, "I understand that women are protective of their brats, so I will overlook this from you. Shut your ugly face and fix my tortillas. I am hungry now, squaw."

She thought, *The white man does not listen or learn. I will stop him. I will win this battle if I should have to kill him this very moment.* Coyote Hunter spoke, "If you overlook it, you will die, husband. I will always be watching. You will not have an opportunity to make the child fear you or to place fear in her heart for me. I know your ways, and they are not good. You will not touch Prairie Blossom in any manner. Do you understand me?"

Her husband felt an odd kind of hurt in his heart. He thought of how could she hate him so after all he had done for her? He scratched the hard ground for her and now for the brat. He made up his mind that from this moment on, she could find her own food.

He shouted, "Feed yourself and the brat! Don't look to me when your belly is empty." He leaped out of bed and flew through the creaking door of the hut.

Coyote Hunter whispered, "I already do, husband. I already do." She was relieved. It was over, and she knew that he understood completely. She knew his nature though. It did not mean that he would not die. He was a very stubborn white man. She told herself to always remain vigilant. He had received more than the coyotes she hunted. He had received a life-threatening warning.

Chapter Four

Mitch did not leave the hut in fear. He left in a black rage. He thought, *Coyote Hunter has no right to tell me I cannot touch that brat. I will touch her! She is as much my property as her mother's. I am the man around here. I give the orders, not her. Coyote Hunter will do as I say.* As he walked through the cornfield, he was thinking of ways to get out of this dilemma while bringing Coyote Hunter back under his thumb. He knew she had gone crazy, but when? Was it when the baby was born? Or was she always crazy?

He was perplexed. He thought, *I know I hit her sometimes, but all women have to put up with some slapping around. That was only part of being a woman. All in all, I feel that I have been pretty good to her. I don't make her work the fields, do I? She is just a squaw, and she is playing like she is the kind of woman you have to treat and talk to special like.*

As he thought, his black hearted desires came to the front of his mind. He had decided to take the easiest way out. She and the brat weren't worth anymore of his efforts. Life had been so much simpler looking out after himself. This decision settled his problem; he needed to get rid of her and the brat. He would write them off as a bad bargain. He knew it didn't pay to trade with Apaches; they will cheat you in a second. Now that he thought of it, he was sure the Apaches knew she was crazy when they traded her. Why else would their Medicine Man discuss their hitchin' privately with Coyote Hunter? She was just another squaw. He bet they laughed at him when they ate his horsemeat.

He had to admit, it was partly his fault; he had to have her when he caught sight of her bathing in the pond, nearly nude. He was sure now the Apaches planted her there for him to see. He could see their plan clearly now. He had been set up. He saw only her beauty. He saw sunlight and the sparkling water flowing over her breasts and belly. He could still see that first sight of her in his mind. The memory brought a small pang, a feeling of regret and loss. He had to admit, there were some things he would miss about Coyote Hunter.

Mitch was determined that he would get back from the Apaches what belonged to him. He would steal that mound of coyote furs she had stashed under her traveling gear. He had also noticed a short spear, made for a woman. He wondered what kind of woman he had received in the trade deal. Whatever she was, it was evident that she had been holding back from him. He wondered why she would do such a thing. He had done all he could to be good to her.

His decision was made. All his mind thought about was killing Coyote Hunter. His own heart would betray him. He would know this for a brief time.

Mitch decided to follow her. He would kill her on the Apache Trail. He chuckled. He would take all of the hides she planned to give to the Apaches. He would laugh at the Apaches as they had laughed at him. He would leave the Injun papoose for the wild animals and the elements. The papoose was only a half breed; she did not matter much as far as Mitch was concerned.

Mitch was sure-fire certain that Coyote Hunter would never suspect that he had decided to kill her. His skinning knife should be enough; after all, she was only a weak squaw. His skinning knife was razor-sharp, and he carried it in a case on his belt. He should catch up to her in a day. He would only take one full canteen. He reasoned that he would have no weight to carry and that he would make better time than her. He was sure he would be back the next morning.

Mitch came back to the hut and discovered that Coyote Hunter had already left on her journey. He wished that she was still here; he would have killed her right then. He was consumed with bloodlust. As usual, she had to make things more difficult for him.

He filled his canteen and scowled in aggravation as he moved to leave the wobbly hut. He slammed the rickety door behind him.

Coyote Hunter heard the slam and knew of his anger. She was not far up the trail. She thought once more, *Be vigilant*.

Chapter Five

Coyote Hunter had been on the trail for several hours. She was nearly one-half of the way to the Apache camp. It was much harder trotting across the prairie with the baby and all the gifts she had prepared for the Apache Chief and the Medicine Man. She would have to rest soon. The babe needed an uninterrupted feeding and a change of coyote fur. She located an elevated shelter of rocks that provided a yawning vast amount of deep shade. She stopped there to rest and croon to the babe as she nursed. Prairie Blossom had not cried through the trot on the hot, dusty, and long trail. Coyote Hunter thought to herself, *She will be a resource to the people. She will also be the discernible source of my motherly pride.* She laughed out loud at her thoughts. She was sure that all mothers had these feelings about their papooses.

Coyote Hunter was proud of her accomplishments. She had over two hundred hides, and all were tanned perfectly. She had brushed them into a luxurious luster. They would feed the people as trade items for many moons.

Unfortunately, her husband cast covetous eyes on them this morning. She saw his eyes gleam as he calculated their worth to the whites. He was very close to learning her secret. She saw that she must be more careful.

Coyote Hunter lay Prairie Blossom in a safe place and looked for firewood to cook her supper. She was ravenous. She found a cache of sticks another traveler had left. It was Coyote Hunter's turn to fill the cache for the next traveler. It was simple courtesy.

A movement caught her eye; she noticed a speck down the trail. It must be the man who was her husband. So, he had decided to follow her. Coyote Hunter could feel his hatred this far away; she was sure he had decided to kill her and the babe. Coyote Hunter was not surprised. She would not allow it to happen though. She thought with a deep regret, *It has come down to this between us. I must fight him, and I must kill him. He will always be a danger if I allow him to live.* She could not give him the hides and go back to her people, even though she knew that was all he really wanted. If she did that, she would be trading Prairie Blossom's honor for her life. All Apache knew that life without honor is no life at all. She felt her blood heat. She would fight him, and she would kill him. He would be out of her life forever, and that was what she really wanted.

It was time to make plans. She intended to win this battle. She would make camp in this rock cavern. She would bait him like any other animal she intended to kill. She would make sure he saw her fire and smelled her meat. As she continued to watch him, she noticed that he seemed to be staggering as he walked. She thought, *Surely he hadn't left the hut without adequate supplies.* It was like him to be so cocky; he was always the fool. Another idea occurred to her. He thought she would be so easy to kill, did he? She laughed quietly; her tone was laced with menace. He would die with his stupidity intact and none of her meat or water in his belly. Her husband would approach her thinking her submissive and in fear of him. He would expect that she would tenderly care for him. He would be wrong. She would be vicious in her treatment of him. Apaches despised weakness in their enemy. Her discovery of his weakness and vulnerability would make it that much easier to kill him. He would be easy prey to bring down.

She thought in this life-and-death manner simply because she was a hunter. There was no emotion involved other than hate, vengeance, or survival. Fear did not enter her heart. She was sure she could kill him without any of the advantages he offered her. But it was wise to use them all.

Soon, Mitch zigzagged into her den of rocks as if he belonged there. Coyote Hunter thought, *He shows no dread of me. This is one more fatal mistake on his part.*

He said in a raspy voice, "Water and food, squaw."

Coyote Hunter simply looked at him in innocence and feigned surprise. He gestured angrily toward the meat on the spit and the canteen placed on the rock farthest away and then at her.

Coyote Hunter said, "No, husband. I will not make provision for you, and you will not take any for yourself." She raised her short spear and stamped it on the ground to emphasize her meaning.

Mitch's broken voice said, "Why, Coyote Hunter? I have been good to you."

Coyote Hunter laughed merrily. "You have come here to kill Prairie Blossom and myself. You also intended to take my bundle of furs. Do not lie. I know this to be true in my heart."

Mitch said, "You own nothing, squaw. The furs belong to me. That goes for the brat too. What have you done with the pitiful girl child?"

Coyote Hunter did not answer him. She would never tell him where Prairie Blossom was hidden. She had placed her in a notch in the ceiling of the rock cavern. She would be safe there. She made sure that she did not glance in that direction when her husband queried her. She would retrieve Prairie Blossom when this fight was over. It was imperative that she win; she would use any methods she needed to employ.

Mitch roared loudly and rushed toward Coyote Hunter with his remaining energy. He was reaching for her throat with clawlike fingers. She sidestepped his dash and attempted to place her spear inside his kidney. He was quicker than she thought. His skinning knife was in his hand in less than a breath. He began the dance of the knives. He rapidly slashed outward and cut her right upper arm. It was not a life-threatening wound, but she was losing much blood.

She continued to circle with him, her spear poised for stabbing. She had never fought a man, but she knew survival depended on her not giving ground. She must stand.

She began to think as all woman think in any life-or-death situation. *I must wait for his next strike to give him overconfidence. He will think he can kill me at his leisure.*

He lunged again, low. He cut her left arm a bit lower. He did not notice that she did not dodge his thrust. She simply raised her arm. She knew he was attempting to cut her arteries. He meant for her to bleed to death.

The dance of the knives was tiring her. She had been burdened throughout her long trot that day. And he was still very strong. She had underestimated his strength. She thought, *For Prairie Blossom's sake, I must end this soon. I cannot hold out much longer. But how can I kill him?* Suddenly, his largest weakness came to her woman's mind. She stepped close to him with her spear held loosely.

He thought, *Coyote Hunter is giving in rather than die by my knife.*

She said in her softest voice, "Mitch, I do love you. You can have the hides and me." She knew he had never been loved in his horrid life. She spoke in her softest voice, letting him see a gentleness that glowed brightly from her sharp black eyes.

His attack upon her ceased abruptly. Her soft words brought him into a hopeful and dreamy state of mind. He became soft and malleable in her hands. She stepped close to him while continuing to smile as she recognized the anticipation shining brightly in his bright blue eyes. As she kissed his lips, she poised her spear. He did not notice. He was gazing into her black deceitful eyes with shining hope. He truly believed her love was in his grasp. Her opportunity had come.

She thrust upward, with all the strength her small body possessed, into his beating heart. He was dead before his body landed on the floor of the rock cavern.

Coyote Hunter's body sagged in relief.

She dragged his familiar body far from the rock cavern with her remaining strength. She would leave his body for the wild animals to ravage, as she had vowed. She placed his hat with the rattle skin band back on his head and straightened his clothes. She spoke one last time to him in a tone laced without the smallest amount of sadness.

She said, "Goodbye, husband."

She turned and walked to her cavern to remove Prairie Blossom from her hiding place and to eat, to drink, and to clean her hunting spear. During this time, she felt no sorrow or guilt. Her blood was still high. She saw it as a necessary kill. It was between her and her husband.

However, Coyote Hunter knew she must return to the Apache village and confess this matter to the Great Chief as soon as she could. Confession was her duty.

As her blood cooled, Coyote Hunter was starting to see the seriousness of her actions and how they would be viewed by her people. Apache law was clear. A woman was forbidden to fight, except in war. Her duty then was to defend her Brave's back. Coyote Hunter had broken the law and fought a man, her own husband.

She fervently hoped that the Great Chief would understand and that the Medicine Man would intercede on her behalf. She reasoned that all Apache saw that the Great Chief was a fighter for his people and had been hunted by the white man many times. He would see the dilemma her husband had brought to her and her mother's need to save Prairie Blossom. He would see that she had run before she fought him. He would see he intended to kill her and the babe.

Out of anxiety, Coyote Hunter spoke, "Oh, surely he would see that I had no other choice."

Chapter Six

Coyote Hunter did not sleep that night. She was haunted by the memory of the bright shining hope in her husband's light eyes. She would never forget that sight, even though she was only sixteen years old. It taught her something about herself; his hope had not stayed her hand. Was there no softness in her heart? She knew she had always despised him, and she had learned she was capable of a killing hate for another human being. Intentionally, she had killed her husband. Her feelings were an overwhelming hate and satisfaction as she drove her spear into his heart. Her spirit soared the very instant she felt her spear pierce his heart.

Regret for her actions came once her Apache blood cooled. Coyote Hunter could not understand why she regretted his loss. She was young; she had not learned that it is a woman's way to regret loss of all kinds. Especially if another's death is necessary for your own survival. She only knew that her conscience felt the need to be punished or absolved. She must confess and humbly accept the just punishment from her people.

When the sun rose from behind the clouds, she woke Prairie Blossom and nursed her. She hitched on her pack and began the remainder of the long trot to her tribe. She did not stop to look at what was left of her husband. She didn't think she could bear another memory. She needed the heartfelt cleansing she would receive after the judgment of the Great Chief.

She trotted all day and reached her people at dusk. She was so emotionally forlorn, she burst into tears upon seeing them. She could not talk; she could only weep. Bright Star, her mother, ran to her and escorted her to the Medicine Man's lodge. She knew Coyote Hunter best, and she knew there was a serious matter to be resolved. She was very apprehensive; she knew this could have disastrous consequences. Bright Star thought, *What has Coyote Hunter done?* She prayed for Coyote Hunter and for herself. *Please, Great Spirit, do not let me lose my daughter and my new granddaughter. I have lost one child in the white man wars. Please show forgiveness to the only child left to me. Please do not take her from me. Oh, Great Spirit, Coyote Hunter is only a child and prone to make mistakes. Please, Great Spirit. Forgive my daughter for her wrong.* In anger, she shouted toward the heavens, "Have I not borne enough in this life, Great Spirit? Please, Great Spirit, forgive her!" She then ceased her prayers. She had no hope that they had been heard. She felt in her heart that she would lose her daughter. She was overcome with desolation. She had done all a woman could do, pray and prepare herself for another loss in her short life.

Chapter Seven

Coyote Hunter bowed low enough for her chin to touch the floor when she entered the Medicine Man's lodge. She was displaying her grief and fear with an uncontrolled great whooping.

He said kindly, "Hush now, child. Drink this tea, and then you may tell your story."

She drank the bitter tea; her wailing ceased immediately.

He said, "Now, you may tell your story, child."

She began haltingly from the beginning. She said, "My husband beat me many times. He was angry because his work on his farm was fruitless and unrewarding. He blamed me." She paused to see if the Medicine Man would speak. He did not speak. She continued, "He struck me with his fist on the day Prairie Blossom was born. He was angry because I gave birth to a girl child." She paused again, hoping he would say something sympathetic or even show his feelings with a gesture. He spoke no words and made no gestures. As he listened to her words, his expression reflected a penetrating concentration.

She spoke of her greatest fear. The Medicine Man saw her fear was the motivation that had compelled her to do all the wrong things she had done. Coyote Hunter began to confess, her need for absolution reflected on her beaten face. She admitted that she had disrespected her husband based on her fear that he would harm the babe. Her fear was so great, she was driven by her mother's heart to threaten her husband with death if he ever touched the babe. This fearfulness was the reason she made the decision to bring Prairie Blossom to her people for the Medicine Man's blessing at the babe's young age. As a mother, she felt she needed to remove Prairie Blossom far away from her husband's fists and to a safe place.

She then revealed to the Medicine Man that she had left at dawn for the Apache camp under very bad circumstances. Her husband did not even see her leave. The Medicine Man did wonder what kind of husband would not accompany his wife on such a harsh trip. However, this thought did not show in his eyes or on his face. The Medicine Man composed a mental note to reflect on these revelations.

Coyote Hunter continued to confess. She said, "At the one-half-way mark on the trail leading to the Apache village, I noticed that my husband was following. He was staggering, back and forth, across the prairie trail. I was sure then that he had left our hut in a rage and without adequate supplies. My rage flared up and burned great. I felt like the game I myself hunted. I was sure he intended to kill me and Prairie Blossom and to take the hides I had prepared as a birth gift to the people."

The Medicine Man thought, *As any mother, she wished to bring honor to Prairie Blossom. With these thoughts, she was overcome with hate for him. She made the decision to use this staggering weakness against him.*

She confessed to the Medicine Man that she baited her husband with meat and water, but she never intended to give him either. She only meant to bring him into her rock cavern. Rage led her to believe it was necessary to kill him to keep her own life and to save Prairie Blossom's life.

She relayed that he staggered into her rock cavern demanding water and food. She refused him. He became angry and approached the dripping meat and took note of the cool water in the canteen.

Coyote Hunter spoke of how she pounded her spear on the ground and said, "No, husband, you will not have any." He then snarled and attacked her. She was poised and ready.

She paused a moment to regain her composure while confessing her actions. Once composed, she began the tale of her battle with him. She fought her husband as a man would fight another man, the dance of the knives. She told of his strength and that he had drawn first blood from her. She told of how she was tiring rapidly in this life-and-death battle and knew she would lose the fight if she continued to fight him on equal footing as a man.

Coyote Hunter said how her woman's mind began to search for a survival tactic, and it came to her. Her mind thought to bait him again. This time, she used something she knew he needed desperately—her love and respect. She pretended to end the fight by using sweet words and an earnest expression, and she told of how his light eyes began to shine with hope. His reaction did not touch her heart; her Apache blood was too high. She only felt a sense of triumph. She let her spear dangle loosely and maneuvered close to him. She poised her spear in an instant and stabbed upward with all her strength directly into his heart.

She expressed how her hate magnified tenfold for her husband as his blood dripped down her arm. She divulged how that same blood brought her a feeling of sweet vengeance. She revealed that she dragged his body outside, far from her rock cavern for the wild animals to ravage. She felt great satisfaction at this action; it felt right to her. He deserved no more; he deserved no honor for the dead.

Once her blood cooled, she felt only regret for her actions. She was haunted by the sight of his light eyes that had overflowed with shining hope. She ended by saying, "I had no choice. I had to kill him or be killed by him." Tears of sorrow bathed her face as she finished her story.

The Medicine Man observed she spoke honestly, but with a young woman's and a young mother's viewpoint. He also noticed that the last thing she said was that she had no choice—it was kill him or be killed by him.

The Medicine Man smiled at her kindly. She was still a youth, and all knew that the young are blind.

He said, "I will need to converse with the Great Chief on this matter. You must stay with your mother, and you will have two guards with you at all times. You have freedom of the village as long as you stay with the guards. There is one last thing I wish to say to you. Hear what I say. There is always a choice. Coyote Hunter, we become what we wish to become in the end. You must think very deeply on my words. The wrong you have done will become apparent to you. You will acknowledge the reasons for your regret and pain. Only then will your punishment be accepted in your heart. Only then will your consciousness heal. You may go now."

As Coyote Hunter left the Medicine Man's lodge, two guards were waiting. They lined up on either side of her as she walked. They were carrying their spears in an aggressive manner. She thought, *How did they know? How do they know what I have done?* They did not speak; they simply escorted her to her mother's lodge.

Chapter Eight

Coyote Hunter walked to her mother's lodge with the guards walking close beside her. The people stared and whispered behind their hands. She knew they were wondering what trouble she had caused and why she needed to be guarded. They suddenly became fearful of her as they watched her pass by. All of them recognized that Coyote Hunter could bring her bad luck onto them. They did not speak to her, and they cast their eyes down as she passed.

Coyote Hunter felt hot tears sting her eyes. She did not allow them to fall out of dogged pride. She loved the people; they would not change their beliefs even though they had known her all her life. Coyote Hunter had done the same to others awaiting the tribunal. Apache law was very fair and very strict; it had to be if the people were to live peacefully among themselves.

Upon reaching her mother's lodge, one of the guards rapped on the door with his spear. Coyote Hunter's mother must have been waiting. She yanked the door open immediately. She was holding Prairie Blossom to her breast. She did not understand why her daughter was guarded, but she did not ask. She knew it was serious. She thanked the guards for bringing her beloved daughter to her pitiful lodge.

She took Coyote Hunter by the arm and pulled her roughly inside. The blood began to flow again. The guards placed themselves on either side of the door. Coyote Hunter's mother shut the door respectfully.

Bright Star turned to Coyote Hunter with a very sad expression. She said, "I have been praying for my one child to be forgiven. What have you done, Coyote Hunter? Please tell your mother. I will know then if my prayers have been in vain. Have no fear for me. I have prepared myself for the worst." As she spoke, she bandaged Coyote Hunter's arm with prairie lint held in place with useless pieces of buffalo hide. Soon, the flow of blood ceased.

Coyote Hunter sighed in resignation. She knew she had to tell her mother. She did not want to, but her mother took her in and had a right to know. She said, "I will tell you everything that I told the Medicine Man, Mother."

When Coyote Hunter finished the story, Bright Star began to weep and wail. She beat on her breast with all her might. The pain of losing another child was unendurable; she wished she could stop her heart from beating one more time. She discerned she would lose this child and her grandchild. She knew the laws her people lived by. She saw that this child had committed a terrible deed. But this was her beloved child.

Coyote Hunter dropped to her knees and laid her head in her mother's lap.

Bright Star said, "My prayers have been in vain. It is a terrible occurrence, Coyote Hunter. Think! Could you not have outrun him? Could you not have allowed the Braves to stop him when you arrived? The Great Spirit gave you the gift of running. You could have saved yourself and Prairie Blossom from the fate that awaits you now. Oh, Coyote Hunter, why did you confront your husband when it was truly not a necessary thing to do? That is how the Medicine Man and the Great Chief will see it, and they will be right, Coyote Hunter."

Coyote Hunter said, "I see that now, Mother. I did not see it before. I only knew that my blood ran hot. I did not think or control myself. You are right, Mother, and so is the Medicine Man. He told me I did have a choice. You have made me see that was true. He also told me that we all become what we want to be in the end. It is true. My blood only wanted to kill him, and I became a killer. I deserve punishment for what I have done. I will not shame you when it is given to me. Mother, please forgive me?"

Bright Star laid the babe down. She took Coyote Hunter in her arms and held her as if she was an infant. She said, "I love you, Coyote Hunter. I do forgive you. Never forget these things I say to you. They will give you strength to endure what must be endured. I know you will make me proud when your punishment is announced. You are strong and blessed by the Great Spirit."

Coyote Hunter asked her mother, "Mother, if the punishment should be death, would you take Prairie

Blossom and raise her? Would you teach her about me? Would you tell her how much I loved her?"

Bright Star very solemnly said, "Coyote Hunter, I give my word to do all these things and more. Please, let us not think about death as a punishment. It could be banishment. At the least, I would know that you are alive. Let us think only of banishment."

Coyote Hunter said, "But, Mother, where will I go? What will I do?"

Bright Star said, "You will do what you have done since you were ten years old: you will hunt. You will go where the Great Spirit leads you. The Great Spirit has not forsaken you, Coyote Hunter. He knows his children make mistakes. He knows your heart and sees that you are repentant. I have taught you this as a child. Has living with the white man caused you to forget?"

Coyote Hunter said, "No Mother, I just needed to hear it again, from you. I am afraid of what my future could be."

Bright Star said, "The Great Spirit makes known his wishes through the Medicine Man. If you are banished, you will be told where to go. And you will be alive, Coyote Hunter. It will not be so bad when you are settled with shelter and meat. You will be happy as you watch Prairie Blossom grow. Listen to your mother's words, you will see."

Chapter Nine

Coyote Hunter stayed with her mother for nearly a week awaiting the tribunal. She would not leave her mother's lodge. She knew the people would not acknowledge her. The pain of her people's loss was great in her heart. She understood that they must not treat her as if she had not done wrong.

Her mother visited each and every lodge and told them what Coyote Hunter had done along with the things the white man had done to her. She reminded them of her beaten face when she came to the tribe. She did this lest they form their own opinions and object to the tribunal's judgment.

All Apache, even women, had a say in the proceedings. All saw that Bright Star was doing what was best for her precious child. She subtly encouraged banishment at each lodge. The disgruntled and hard-hearted Apaches informed the Medicine Man of her activities.

He said, "I will tell each and every one of you, I see no harm in her. She wants her child to live. Any parent would do the same."

THE CHOSEN ONES

Coyote Hunter knew that her mother was doing the best she could for her. It was awkward for Coyote Hunter. She could see what a fool she had been. Her mother did not present her as one. Her mother stressed her youth and that she had made a terrible mistake.

Coyote Hunter knew now that she should have run from her husband. She could have outrun him easily, even with the loads of Prairie Blossom, the supplies, and the hides. Running like the wind was the Great Spirit's gift to her. She spurned it when she chose to fight her husband. She used deceit to bait him and to kill him. She still saw his light shining hopeful eyes in her sleep at night. She wondered if the memory of those eyes would ever go away.

The drums thumped loudly for a short period. It was the sign for all Apaches to stop and listen.

The Great Chief walked from his lodge to the middle of the camp. He said, "The Medicine Man and I will carry out the tribunal for Coyote Hunter. It will be at moonrise. We will hear your disagreements at this time. As always, the Medicine Man and your Great Chief make the final decision on Coyote Hunter's fate. You who wish to speak, place yourself in Coyote Hunter's moccasins. You may go."

Bright Star was thrilled at this announcement. The Great Chief had all but said banishment and told the others to think of it as if they were in Coyote Hunter's moccasins. This was a very good sign.

Coyote Hunter had not been informed, but Bright Star had decided to leave the tribe and go with her precious child. She would not allow her only child or her grandchild to leave her forever.

Bright Star had nothing she regretted leaving. Her husband had died in the white man's wars. She wanted to see something different than the hard-baked prairie. Her daughter would be concerned, but she would be happy.

Bright Star thought, *Coyote Hunter will not go alone. I will not have her face the unknown without her mother. I am only a widow in this camp. Yet I am a young woman, only thirty-two turns of the circling sun. My hair is long and black. My eyes are sharp and dark. I am slender and strong. I am still lovely. I will go and hope for a new love.*

Coyote Hunter heard the Great Chief's announcement from her mother. She was hopeful for the first time. She smiled at her mother with a dancing light in her eyes.

Her mother said, "I have another announcement for you."

Coyote Hunter said, "What is it, Mother?"

Bright Star said, "I am going with you and the babe. You are not leaving without me."

Coyote Hunter was surprised to find out that her mother was actually looking forward to banishment. However, she was thrilled to know she would have her family with her. She ran and jumped in her mother's lap, like a child, and held Bright Star around the neck. She said, "Oh, Mother, are you sure? I don't want you to do something you don't want to do."

Her mother laughed. "I am thrilled to go. I am stagnating here. I need new experiences in my life."

They laughed, hugged each other, and began to pack up.

CHAPTER TEN

The Great Chief Eagle Heart entered with great grandeur into the tribunal meeting ground. His steps were akin to the beat of the drums. It was a Great Chief's duty to impress the people. He must bring to the fore their respect for the tribunal's trial.

His attire was striking. His entire headdress consisted of feathers from his hunts and subsequent capture of numerous white majestic eagles. The white eagle was a great kill. This kill brought much status to the victorious hunter. The white eagle was rare, large, strong, and had much intelligence.

The length of the Great Chief's headdress was great. It stretched far to his ankles and trailed far behind him as he walked through the ceremonial grounds with immeasurable dignity. The tips of the feathers had been dyed a dark red to symbolize the eagles' life gift of blood. The Apaches believed wholly that upon an eagle's death, the eagle's qualities were transmitted to the victorious hunter. The Great Chief radiated the qualities of the eagle's keen sight, swiftness in battle, and his innate magnificence.

This brought the Great Chief ample admiration from the people. Thus, peace and self-gratification resided within his heart. He was wise, past his prime, and forgiving. These qualities would benefit Coyote Hunter.

Coyote Hunter's spear was decorated with eagle feathers. She carried it now, but in her left hand, showing respect and honor for the Great Chief. He had given her the eagle feathers decorating her spear during the ceremony presenting her to the spirits as Coyote Hunter. She was a woman, yet she carried eagle feathers. It was a great honor. One she feared she was going to lose.

Tears sprang into Coyote Hunter's eyes, but she continued to study the Great Chief through her tears. She hoped to perceive the Great Chief's intentions of her fate.

She noticed he was clad in deerskin tunic and leggings decorated with beads. These beads were in many different patterns that displayed the many great deeds the Great Chief had executed in his life. Coyote Hunter understood the extent of his wisdom compiled through experience. She thought, *He is very impressive. I have never been near enough to see the beaded drawings before. I see that he has done many great things for the Apache nation. What will he think of me? I am insignificant in comparison.*

Coyote Hunter watched the Great Chief seat himself on a stool encased with black bear fur. Over the edge of the stool's seat lay the bear's head. Its mouth was open, displaying its intimidating teeth. Coyote Hunter felt even more insignificant. She thought, *I have never killed an animal larger than a coyote. I see there is no bravery or honor to be bestowed in the kill of a small coyote.* She did not see the privilege given to her by the Great Spirit as she fed the tribe during the years of famine when all other animals had left in search of water. It was fortunate for her that the Great Chief and the Medicine Man did see her contribution.

Coyote Hunter's mind was racing as she stood in the circle of judgment, to the left of the Great Chief. The Medicine Man and Magic Man were standing in the circle to his right, the position of honor and power. The Magic Man was also clad impressively. His deerskins were stained with berry juice with drawings of the sun, moon, stars, and many other mysterious symbols. The meanings were known only to the Magic Man. The Medicine Man wore the White Buffalo crown, horns protruding from the sides. His ceremonial hand-carved granite knife was wedged between his beaded belt and his deerskins. It was visible for all to see; it was meant to be. The holy knife was deadly sharp. It was used when the penalty issued by the Great Chief was death. If it was used, death became a permanent state. The spirits turned away from you forever. A fearsome death and one not expended lightly. Coyote Hunter thought, *I have committed a terrible act. I deserve the penalty of the knife.*

Moonrise lit up the sky in a violet haze. Coyote Hunter felt her palms become slick, and small beads of sweat broke out on her upper lip. It was unknown to Coyote Hunter, but the Medicine Man and the

Great Chief had decided Coyote Hunter's fate several days earlier. However, the law required that the people had the right to speak in tribunal. The Medicine Man would debate with the people if it became necessary. He would convince the people that the decision made by the Great Chief was correct.

The stars began to glow with small pinpricks of light in the violet sky. Coyote Hunter wondered if it would be the last time she saw this beauty and if she would see Prairie Blossom's face again.

There was the sound of beating drums and then abrupt total silence. The Medicine Man let the silence continue for some moments. The suspense was building in the hearts of everyone.

The Medicine Man announced in a loud deep voice, "Apache people, it is moonrise and time to begin the tribunal. It is time to judge Coyote Hunter for her crimes." He stepped into the speaking circle. He was in view of all. He began to address the people. His first duty was to summarize why they were called to this tribunal.

He said, "Apache people, one of our sisters has committed a grievous offense against our law, and she must be given an appropriate punishment."

Coyote Hunter did not allow the tears to fall from her eyes. She thought, *I never thought I would be standing here. I have always strived to do the right thing. When my character was tested, I failed.*

Her mother, Bright Star, looked at her very intensely. She conveyed a message using only a mother's expression. "Be brave, my little one." Coyote Hunter responded. She threw her shoulders back and her chin up. Bright Star was right. Her pride was all she had left; she must keep it when the verdict was given and afterward.

The Great Chief observed this interaction with a smile of approval. It was as if Coyote Hunter could hear him say, "I was young once too, Coyote Hunter. Do not fear. All is not lost to you, even though you fear it is so." Coyote Hunter began to feel her fears relax in the face of such great wisdom.

The Medicine Man gave a litany of all that Coyote Hunter had done. He then methodically stated what she should have done. He said, "Coyote Hunter is young, and all know the young are blind." He paused, and the suspense built again among the people.

Bright Star was apprehensive. The Medicine Man had built a very convincing case against Coyote Hunter. Coyote Hunter appeared to be tranquil in spite of it. Bright Star thought, *I am proud of her. But I feel that Coyote Hunter is giving the impression she knows what the outcome would be of this tribunal. How could she? No one could speak to her prior or during the tribunal. I hope Coyote Hunter has not accepted her death. It will surely welcome her.*

The Medicine Man continued to speak. He emphasized strongly what would happen if the whites learned the truth and Coyote Hunter was allowed to go unpunished. He said, "Our village will be attacked."

The people gasped and murmured. This thought had not occurred to any of them. Yet they did not show fear. It is the Apache way.

THE CHOSEN ONES

The people had discussed Coyote Hunter's position as the days passed while they waited for the tribunal. The people remembered that Coyote Hunter had fed them many times. They began to feel in their hearts that what she did was not so dreadful. After all, he was only another abusive white man. This attitude spurred from the white man's treatment of the Apache. The people had been harmed by the whites many times. They remembered Coyote Hunter's battered face when she arrived. It had been debated around many campfires. None of the people believed Coyote Hunter should die.

Bright Star had done her work well.

The Medicine Man did not mention death to the people. He appealed to the people's reasoning powers. He said, "If we exile Coyote Hunter, the white man will pursue her. Our village will be safe."

The people accepted the Medicine Man's way out; they wished to believe in their continued safety. They agreed that it was necessary for Coyote Hunter to leave their camp. If she was not here, the whites would hunt her, but never find her. All the people knew that the whites would be sent in the wrong direction. Coyote Hunter was still an Apache. They believed the whites would leave once they knew of her exile. The whites were familiar with Apache ways. They knew exile was an intense punishment that recognized the member as a criminal. Usually, it was a very slow death sentence. The people were sure the camp would be safe if the whites came for Coyote Hunter and she was in exile.

The people began to shout, "Exile, exile, exile!" with one voice. They turned their backs on Coyote

Hunter and crossed their arms. They kept their backs to her and waited for their dismissal from the Great Chief.

He nodded to the Medicine Man, who said, "Apache people. Please go home to your beds. Thank you for such a wise decision."

The Great Chief smiled kindly at Coyote Hunter. "Coyote Hunter, you have been exiled by the people's unanimous wish. You may leave with the dawn. You will go north as far into the mountains as is necessary to evade the white man."

Bright Star spoke up, "I will be going with her, Great Chief."

The Great Chief said, "So be it, Bright Star. If you leave, I fear you will not return."

Bright Star said, "Does death stalk me, Great Chief?"

The Great Chief said, "It is for the Great Spirit to say, Bright Star. We all must die someday. You are Apache. Die with bravery and honor. I bid you farewell." He turned and walked with a sad expression back to his lodge.

Bright Star felt a cold shiver run through her body. Yet she would not leave her child and grandchild to face what lay in the north. She would go and die if she must. She would follow her destiny.

Chapter Eleven

Coyote Hunter and Bright Star went to the lodge. Coyote Hunter curled up in front of the burning hearth. She wept like a small child.

Bright Star was alarmed. "Why do you weep, my child? You have your life."

Coyote Hunter said, "I am no longer an Apache, Mother."

Bright Star said, "It is true that you are an exiled Apache, but you will always be Apache, Coyote Hunter. It is your bloodline. That cannot be changed. Do you think your hair will change to yellow and your eyes turn light? All will always see you as an Apache. Do you not understand?"

Coyote Hunter stopped weeping and said, "That is true, Mother. I will always be Apache. Tell me, Mother, have we finished packing for the dawn?"

Bright Star said, "Yes, my child. I have packed things for Prairie Blossom too."

Coyote Hunter said, "Mother, I heard what the Great Chief foretold. You need not go with us. I would not want you with us if going would mean your death."

Bright Star said, "No, my child. He also said that we all die sometime. That could mean I die of the white man's sickness in this camp. I prefer to die with glory and honor."

Coyote Hunter answered her simply, "Sleep well, Mother. Thank you for accompanying me. I value you. Please take care."

Bright Star said, "Good night. May the Great Spirit guard your dreams, my dear child."

Chapter Twelve

The dawn broke with a rosy radiance as the moon descended beyond the ends of the earth. Coyote Hunter nursed Prairie Blossom, and her mother gathered all their packs together. They were ready before the sun peeked fully over the horizon.

Bright Star prayed to the Great Spirit for his blessing on their journey. They examined everything in the lodge for the last time. Both knew it would belong to another soon. They had ensured that all was orderly for the next occupant. Bright Star felt no regrets; it had sheltered her for many moons. Now it would shelter others.

It was nearly dawn. They loaded themselves with all their packs. Bright Star thought, *The packs are heavy, but they will soon lighten.* She did not know the full truth of her words. They lifted the hide door and left the lodging.

When they stepped outside, the Medicine Man was mounted and holding two more horses. They were fresh and spirited mares, brown like the forest trees. The Medicine Man was having some slight difficulty holding his stallion. He was a large white gold-spotted stallion, and he was ready to gallop with the wind spirits.

He said rapidly, "The whites are close behind you, and they are mounted. You must take these horses. Quickly! Place your packs on the horses."

Coyote Hunter and Bright Star obeyed with agility. When they were done, they looked to him for further instructions.

He said, "The Great Chief wishes that I take you to the secret entrance leading to the north. You will have no chance otherwise. The people will muddle your tracks, and you will follow behind me. I have prayed to the wind spirits to carry you on. Do not stop, the whites are deadly. I must tell you, Bright Star, your bravery is not in question. You need not go. The hidden trail can be followed easily by Coyote Hunter."

Bright Star said, "I will outwit these white men, Medicine Man. I have no fear. The Great Spirit is with me. I will fulfill my destiny. Is it not the Apache way?"

The Medicine Man said proudly, "Come, mount up and let us leave the white man far behind."

As they passed through the village, the people were riding several horses back and forth in order to confuse and mislead the whites. Many of the Braves called out to them to have courage as they galloped past them. The people's actions left no doubt in Coyote Hunter's mind that they would give their very own lives to save them. Their Apache blood was high, and it generated a great rage that bore no trace of cowardice. Oh yes, the people were sure the whites would challenge them. This gave the people great pleasure. The Apache planned to outwit them and thwart the capture of Bright Star and Coyote Hunter.

Coyote Hunter felt tears sting her eyes. She would never see the faces of her people again. The wind spirits were carrying them rapidly, the people's faces were blurred, and Coyote Hunter wished for one more genuine view of her people. Her tears flowed; she was remorseful. She had brought the white man upon her innocent people. Her mother had assured her that she would always be Apache. This was the proof she needed. There would be no betrayal. All knew Apache would give their lives for their tribal members. This thought brought pride to the front. Her tears stopped their flow. It was time to put aside her grief and emulate the bravery displayed by her people.

The Medicine Man soon came to a sudden halt; his horse reared with the effort. Coyote Hunter's and Bright Star's horses soon followed his example.

He said, "Do you see between the two large boulders? There is a trail behind the brush. That is the secret entrance to the north. I do not know if the white man knows of it. Two complete sunrises from here will bring you to a large forest. You may stop and drink at a large lake. Ride all night. The whites will catch you if you do not. I must tell you, it is not a pleasant thing to be caught by the whites. You have seen this in your life, Bright Star? If you must kill one, take their clothing, all of it. You did not do that, Coyote Hunter? But you are not a killer of men, so you would not know. You must go now. I must go back to the village. I am needed there. Do as I say, and you may live."

He then spoke directly to Coyote Hunter. "Listen closely to this prophecy. It is important that Prairie Blossom live. She is necessary to the future of the people. I will speak no more." He spun his horse toward the village and rode off on the air spirit's back. He was soon out of sight.

Bright Star said, "You must live for Prairie Blossom, Coyote Hunter. Never forget the Medicine Man's prophecy and always remember his holy words. Prairie Blossom is important to the people's future. I must lead the whites away from you. It is the Great Spirit's reason I have come." She called out to Coyote Hunter, "Go now! I will lead those light eyes a chase they have never ran before." She spoke with great anticipation. "Coyote Hunter, you must go now! This is my destiny, and I wish to fulfill it. Go!" Bright Star saw that she must speak tenderly. "I am your mother, Coyote Hunter. Stop sitting on that horse and looking at me with such despondency! You may be sure that I will die with honor and dignity. I will watch over you from the Spirit World. Go now! I love you both."

Bright Star threw back her shoulders with pride as befits a chosen one of the Great Spirit. Her name was placed in a special place within the Spirit World. She kicked her horse into a gallop and rode the wind spirits. She laughed with wild abandon, shouting, "It is a good day to die, my dear daughter!"

All knew it was the Apache way to meet their deaths with joy, dignity, and bravery.

Coyote Hunter saw that Bright Star was leaving the needed tracks. Her action would mislead the whites and protect her daughter and her granddaughter. Coyote Hunter and Prairie Blossom meant more to her than Bright Star's life meant to her. Coyote Hunter knew the whites would follow Bright Star's tracks, and she would be captured. Tears escaped Coyote Hunter and rolled down her face.

Prairie Blossom nudged her breast with her tiny head as if to say "Hurry, we must leave now." Coyote Hunter knew she must go north, or her mother's sacrifice would be worth nothing. Prairie Blossom would not fulfill her destiny, she would die, and her people would die. But it was so hard to watch her mother gallop with such lack of inhibition, knowing she rode to her death.

Coyote Hunter finally accepted Bright Star's last act of love and obeyed her command. She turned her mare to the north.

Chapter Thirteen

Coyote Hunter guided her horse between the large boulders and through the concealing bush. She spurred her mare into a gallop and rode the wind spirits. She wept as she rode for the loss of her mother and the cruelty she must have experienced before she died. Coyote Hunter knew the moment she died, Bright Star touched her spirit with a sense of triumph. She had won her battle even though she had given her life.

Coyote Hunter had not thought about this prophecy concerning Prairie Blossom. She was full of much grief for her mother. She did think now. It was important enough to her mother to give her life for Prairie Blossom. She thought, *How the prophecy will come about, only the Great Spirit knows.* She thought deeper. What was her responsibility in the fulfillment of this prophecy? The answer came to her, and she chuckled at the undemanding solution. She thought, *My role is to teach Prairie Blossom the ways of the Apache. She will then be prepared to step into her role as a Holy Woman to the Apache Nation. The first time I gazed into her eyes, I knew she carried a knowing soul. I will prepare her well. We will ride as the Medicine Man advised us. We will hunt for shelter near a river so I may spear fish. If it proves to be safe, we will stay. I will begin by speaking to her, revealing stories of the Apaches to the babe. She is intuitive. She will understand.*

Coyote Hunter rode from two sunrises through two moonrises. She began to look for a river. She followed the tracks of the animals. They would drink from the river and provide her diet with more than speared fish. She saw no danger in this; she was still so young.

A hunting party belonging to the Black Hills Tribe came from the ambiguous trees and surrounded her before she knew what was happening. There were many Braves, all carrying spears. Their Medicine Man was with them wearing the black buffalo headdress.

Coyote Hunter attempted to run them down with her mare. They laughed as they grabbed her horse's mane and stopped her charge. She groped for her spear. She leapt from her mare and swung her spear in a circle. She was sure she would die, but she would die with honor like her mother. What was it her mother said? Oh yes. "Today is a good day to die." Those words gave her bravery.

She thrust her spear at every warrior who came near. She bared her teeth and produced intimidating gestures and noises. She was fighting to live, but prepared to die.

A Brave caught her by her beautiful hair and dragged her to their Medicine Man. The babe made not a sound. Coyote Hunter thought, *She knows we are in danger.*

The Medicine Man watched her struggles but did not laugh as the Braves mocked her. The Medicine Man said, "Are you the exiled Bedonkohe Apache woman who killed the white man with only a small spear?"

Coyote Hunter was wrestling to get away from the Brave who had her hair.

The Medicine Man said, "Let her go. She will not run. She has a babe in that sling. She will bargain for the child's life at the expense of her own. Let her go now."

The Brave let her go. She stood in the center of the circle. She was holding her spear and showing her courage to die. She answered the Medicine Man, "Yes, I am the woman who killed the white man with this spear."

The Braves guffawed.

The Medicine Man brought his arm down sharply for silence. All became quiet. He asked Coyote Hunter, "How did you kill a man, even a white one, with that small spear?"

Coyote Hunter said, "He was an animal. I baited him as one."

The Medicine Man smiled. "You outwitted him. It is the Apache way. The whites are like a disease. They are spreading all over the land. You ended one, and I see that as good. You should not have been exiled. You are welcome in our territory. What is your spirit name?"

She said, "Coyote Hunter."

He said, "I rename you as She Who Dares. It is an honorable name among our people."

Coyote Hunter did abeyance and said, "Thank you, Medicine Man. May my daughter and I live near the river? We will be no trouble to you or your people."

He said, "Hear me, Black Hill Braves, and tell all others, She Who Dares is welcome on our land. She is not to be molested. She is to be assisted. Do you understand?"

An echo of many male voices rang out, "Yes, Great One, it will be as you wish."

A Brave called Shining Star was assigned to take her to the river. He was a handsome man. He was very tall and muscular. His skin was bronze. His hair was to his waist; it was midnight black. His face was tattooed with many mystical symbols. But it was his eyes that attracted her attention. They were pools of black that seemed to carry the secrets of the world inside of them.

He asked, "May I hold Prairie Blossom?" She Who Dares felt a special trust for this Brave. She handed Prairie Blossom to him. He looked in her eyes and held her small hand. He smiled, and the sun brightened. He said, "You have a fine babe." He did not say that Prairie Blossom would be a conjurer. She would need these powers in the role the Great Spirit had given her to perform.

Shining Star was sent to help build her lodge, and he promised to teach her how to hunt the animals in this region. He told her on their first hunt, he would make the first kill, and she would make the second. It was in her heart to do so.

She Who Dares was no longer homeless, but she knew there would be perils in this new land. She was wiser now.

Chapter Fourteen

Shining Star taught her the Black Hills way of lodge building. The lodge was built in ten sunrises. It was placed near the river and a bed of wild daisies. She Who Dares was impressed with Shining Star's thoughtfulness and thoroughness.

He had built it so much sounder than she had expected. It was sturdy, unlike her husband's hut. It was built with logs, wooden doors, and slits for windows. It had a hearth with a smoke hole. Shining Star told her it was for cooking and heating smoke to escape. He used river sand and mud to chink between the logs. The roof was covered with river stones to resist flaming arrows.

He built the lodge using tools of sharpened stones and logs levered against one another to raise them. Not only was the lodge safe, it was very attractive. This lodge was much larger than the Apaches' lodges. As she gazed at it, she felt a pang of sadness. It felt as if a lifetime had passed since she was Coyote Hunter.

Shining Star noticed her despondency. He sought to distract her. "Lodges are built this way because the winters are harsh in the mountains, and you must heat.

They resist the larger animals and the men that pursue men during the moons of famine." He then said, "Now, it is time for your lesson on using the bow. I wish to hunt for our supper, and you will shoot the animal as I shoot by using my second bow. The game will not escape with two great hunters on its trail."

She Who Dares laughed. "I wish to try, Shining Star."

Shining Star took her hunting many times. He taught her how to read animal tracks. He taught her how to kill larger animals with his bow. He made a larger spear for her and a bow with yellow-tipped fletching for her.

She asked, "Why does the arrow fletching have a yellow tip?"

He said, "That is how you know which of the hunting party made the kill. Braves disdain the color of yellow. It will always be your color." He did not mention that he had placed a protective charm on her bow and arrows. He presented the bow and arrows along with the spear. He said, "It is critically important you learn the bow. Some animals cannot be approached or chased to their death."

She asked him, "How did you know I run with the wind spirits?"

He said, "I am a fledgling holy man. I know many things about you. I also know that Prairie Blossom will be a Holy Woman. She will be the first within the Indian Nation. She will do much good for us with the whites. She must be protected. I must stay with you and see that she is safe. The Medicine Man has spoken of this to me. That is why I have built the lodge so big."

She Who Dares knew it was customary for various Indian members to live in the same lodge. All tribes of Indian had a strong moral code. They lived according to the laws the Great Spirit had given them long ago. There would only be love and loving if both parties agreed. She Who Dares thought, *I will not agree. I want no more babies.*

It was as if Shining Star read her mind. He said, "I will not approach you unless you wish it, even though you are very beautiful. My insignificant powers tell me that you will mother no more children. This lack of childrearing is a gift from the Great Spirit. You must teach Prairie Blossom, and so must I."

She said, "Why do you say insignificant powers? You just read my mind! You have many things to teach Prairie Blossom."

He did not answer but looked pleased by her praise. He smiled at her. "She Who Dares has no knowledge of the amount of power that I could summon as a Black Hills Conjurer." It had been decided by the Medicine Man to conceal this fact from her. She would be frightened and never at peace if she knew.

He sensed that She Who Dares was struggling with his decision to remain with her. He could not tell her that it was necessary. Prairie Blossom must be taught the speech of the Spirit World in order to perform the spells of a Conjurer. She needed to be kept safe from those who would kill her for her power. She radiated power even as a helpless infant. He thought,

Prairie Blossom will learn quickly. I must begin to teach her. She will hear me now.

His mind left Prairie Blossom. He began to think of She Who Dares. He thought, *She will come to me soon. She is a woman that needs to be loved by a man. She was not loved by her white husband. She is a fit mate for me. The Great Spirit has given her many talents. I will wait for her to see me as a woman sees a man. It is the Black Hills way.*

Chapter Fifteen

Shining Star rode his black stallion into the village and requested sleeping furs and many other necessary utensils used for daily living. He specified these items be provided by the Black Hills People as gifts. She Who Dares' adopted people gave generously. Black Hills Braves led several loaded pack horses to their new cabin by the river. Shining Star and She Who Dares had been provided with all they needed for a strong start in this new life.

An unexpected gift had been donated by the Medicine Man. The gift was a large bundle of kindling. It was placed with reverence in the hearth by the Braves. Shining Star soon saw it was necessary to explain the significance of this gift to She Who Dares, whose expression was one of confusion.

He told her, "This gift is holy and symbolic. The Black Hills people began its process. The kindling was dried using rare herbs. This curing would bring the scents prevalent within the forest when burned. The fragrant smoke will rise and spread throughout our lodge. It is a wish from the Medicine Man for peace and happiness between us."

She Who Dares saw that the Medicine Man had blessed them heartily. She realized this gift was also meant to convey an unreserved acceptance for her by the Black Hills tribe. This was so unexpected and overwhelming. She could only weep as she lay her head on Shining Star's shoulder. Her relief was great. She did not know how much she needed this acceptance.

Shining Star had known; he had waited for her much-needed tears to flow upon his chest. Each tear soothed the ache in Shining Star's heart.

She calmed soon, but was contemplative. Shining Star heard She Who Dares' thought: *Why would these people be so good to us?*

He smiled. She still did not understand Shining Star's status within the tribe. It was for the best. She must never know. She would fear his teaching of Prairie Blossom.

They began to live in the cabin with a glow of happiness. Each day, they hunted. Prairie Blossom slept peacefully in her sling upon She Who Dares' breast.

Shining Star continued teaching She Who Dares the bow and the spear. It was a mystery to her. She thought, *Why would he teach a woman the use of a bow and spear? A woman could not touch these weapons within the Apache Tribe, except in the case of war. Even then, it was only allowed in extreme cases. She must protect her Brave's back.*

Shining Star caught her thought, but he did not smile. He thought, *Little One, you will die with honor and dignity. You must be prepared to do so. Oh, it is some time away, but it will happen, and I will lose you.*

She Who Dares thought, *Shining Star says there is much for me to learn. I must learn to shoot a bird out of the air with my bow and learn the lunges with the spear. I do hope I will not disappoint Shining Star. He has been so patient.*

He heard her thought, and he smiled. *Little One, you will never disappoint me. You will see. I am the one who will fail you.* This thought expressed his own anxieties for the future.

She saw his sadness. "What have I done wrong this time?" she asked.

He said, "Nothing at all. It was only a random thought passing through my mind."

She said, "So now I bore you?"

He said, "Never, little one. Never."

She Who Dares realized that she was beginning to have feelings of a guarded kind for Shining Star. There was a want for him in her heart. She hoped it would grow and cover all the bad things in her past. Shining Star was such an attractive man. This, though, barely swayed her. It was the gentleness in his eyes that lured her heart. She was fearful, and she kept this feeling of a beginning desire well hidden, or she thought. She felt so protected and so special when he called her little one. He was nothing like her dead husband. He was a true Brave. She knew what the old ones meant now when they spoke of a Brave as standing out from the others. There is a large difference in men. She was just beginning to learn. If she could only trust, she would have him.

They lived like a small family. She tanned the hides of the animals they hunted. He chopped the firewood to keep the hearth burning. She Who Dares quickly learned that they needed a fire in these hills. She sewed warmer clothing using the furs she tanned for them. Shining Star was impressed with her skills and praised her. Her face flushed; she had never received praise from a Brave. His appreciation warmed her heart; she began to sense a kernel of trust for him.

Shining Star created furniture for their lodge; he surprised her with comfortable stools for them both. These stools were large and wide with armrests. It would make it much easier for her to sew. She saw this right away. She would not need to stop to rest as frequently. She thought, *Shining Star is so considerate. These stools are lined with fur and stuffed tightly with the pine needles that fell from the trees.* Shining Star's consideration for her caused her to remember her dead husband. He had not cared that she sat on the dirt floor of the hut to sew and sleep. She was only a woman, considered to be of little value.

She Who Dares was astonished. She thanked Shining Star with a full heart and tears in her eyes. She would have hugged him, but she still did not have the courage.

She Who Dares did see that she and Shining Star were compatible in many ways. She did not know why she could not let go of the bad things in her life. She thought, *She Who Dares, listen to yourself. It takes time.*

You will love him more and more every day. You both have time, and he is a patient Brave. He will wait for you to come to him.

Shining Star heard her thoughts. He thought, *I know my heart. I am in love with She Who Dares, and I must wait for her to love me without fear. I pray in silence all of my thoughts and desires to the Great Spirit. I need the patience she expects from me to help her let loose of the bad things that are holding her back. She Who Dares is the first woman I have loved. I believe that I will be the first man she has loved. I know she did not love her husband. After all, she did kill him. I want to be the first love in her life. I will treat her with respect, as an equal, always. She is the kind of woman who would settle for nothing less.* He wished with all of his heart as he continued to pray silently to the Great Spirit. *Please make this woman I love live a long life.*

However, he knew as a Conjurer that his wish was in vain. It had to be this way in order for Prairie Blossom's future as a Holy Woman to unfold. She was half-white and half-Indian. She was the one foretold of as coming many years ago. It was the only way for destiny to fulfill the future between the white man and the Indian. He must appreciate She Who Dares while she was with him. Tears came into his eyes and nearly coated his cheeks. He stepped outside and chopped firewood.

Chapter Sixteen

She Who Dares did not wish to conceal her love for Shining Star. Her body ached for his loving touch. Yet she continued to hold back; her fears would not let go of her. Shining Star knew of her dilemma. He knew that he had to help her through it if they were to have a future. But how?

After much thought, Shining Star felt that She Who Dares needed to be presented with visual proof of his love. It needed to be beautiful to impress her. He searched the woods, not knowing what he was looking for. He was sure it would present itself. He stumbled over a large grapevine reaching to the top of a tall tree. The beginning was lying across the path his feet had taken. Shining Star said, "Thank you, Great Spirit, for leading this bungling man to the answer."

Shining Star cut the lengths from the grapevine that he would need and took them back to the river beside their land. He began by curing the vines so they would not decay. He formed them into the shape of a heart. He decorated it with mature pine cones, colorful small stones, and dried berries. In the very center, he placed a small carved arrow with an arrowhead and a yellow feather attached to the shaft. He meant it to display his respect for her as a warrior, as a woman, and as a special gift only for her. He had created something that displayed his heart.

He hid it in his area of the lodge. Soon, it would be time to present it to her. Life was habitual that day; he chopped wood, and she sewed. He noticed that she was working diligently at her sewing. He wondered why she was working so hastily, but did not ask.

Prairie Blossom nursed and fell asleep early that night. He examined her for sickness, but her health was good. He thought, *Did she know? She was powerful, and she was exceptional.*

He took his gift from his hiding place. He had put his heart, soul, and many charms into this expression of love for She Who Dares. He stopped and thought, *How do I present it to her? It must be known as a gift of love.* The answer came to him. He would lay it on her sleeping furs. She would not notice. She was tying off her sewing with a bit of rawhide. He laid it softly on her sleeping furs. When she saw his gift, she looked at the grapevine with an expression like that of a startled deer. Tears of happiness began to roll down her cheeks.

He said, "I give you my heart. It is yours, it will always be. I love you, She Who Dares. I do not wish to wait longer for you to love me in return."

She Who Dares gazed at the grapevine heart. She saw the little arrow, and more tears flowed. She looked at him. Love was shining in his eyes with a bit of vulnerability. Her heart immediately offered up all its reservations. She felt love for him overpower her. They beheld each other with soft, desiring, and loving eyes.

She Who Dares held up the bedding fur she had made out of the animals they hunted together. It was large enough for both of them.

Shining Star saw the meaning of this. Tears rolled down his cheeks. He was so relieved; they were of the same mind. He would finally get to hold the woman he loved in his heart, in his arms, and in his bed. He could not stop crying. She Who Dares went to him and held him close. She spoke words of love to him. Shining Star reached out his hand to her. His expression was hopeful and frightened that she would reject him now. She Who Dares smiled and placed her small hand in his rugged one. He picked her up with care in his strong arms, kissed her gently, and lay her down. He settled beside her, giving her room to leave if she wished.

He thought, *I will not force her even though I want her so badly*. He said, "I will always be gentle, She Who Dares. I will love you till death and beyond. You are the first woman that has kept me waiting to embrace you. May I love you with body and soul now?"

She Who Dares touched his bronzed tattooed face with loving fingertips. "I have been waiting for my bad spirits to pass. They have left me with only a bit of grapevine. Love me, my Brave. Please love me now."

By means of those spoken words, they were bound to one another in eyes of the Great Spirit for as long as both shall wish or as long as both shall live. It was the Black Hills way.

Chapter Seventeen

Life settled into a pleasant routine in spite of one unsettled issue between Shining Star and She Who Dares. Her distress came from watching the developing relationship between Shining Star and Prairie Blossom.

Shining Star was beginning to assume the role of a father regarding Prairie Blossom. She Who Dares knew it was blameless, but it appeared that the games he played with Prairie Blossom would be more suited for a much older child. The games they played distressed her. Prairie Blossom was not yet twenty-four moons in age. She Who Dares made her feelings plain. She said, "Shining Star, I do not like these games you play with Prairie Blossom. She is still a babe."

Shining Star said, "Prairie Blossom is an exceptional little girl. She understands my games and cannot wait to play them. They do her no harm and much good."

She Who Dares agreed out of honesty alone. It was true that Prairie Blossom could not postpone sitting on his lap or tagging along beside him. She Who

Dares thought, *Perhaps I am stricken with jealousy. She loves him as much as a father. He has accepted her as his daughter. I must put my feelings aside. I must not interfere in this growing love between them.*

She felt her mother's spirit pass through her. She heard her voice in her heart. She spoke, "Let them have their games, She Who Dares. They are essential for Prairie Blossom's development."

She Who Dares took her mother's words to heart. She knew her mother would not mislead her. She Who Dares would allow the games.

One special game Shining Star played was called Whispering and Listening. He said words in a near silent whisper into Prairie Blossom's ear. In reality, he was teaching her the language of the Spirit World. Prairie Blossom was born with this knowledge as a Conjurer; she only needed reminding as a human. He was melding the two parts of her, human and Conjurer.

Prairie Blossom's lessons were and had always been Shining Star's responsibility. It was a responsibility assigned long ago by the Great Spirit. Shining Star only knew that one would come that he must teach. He did not expect a small babe to enter his life. When he held her in his arms for the first time, he felt a great love overtake him. He examined her and saw that she was exceptional. She was half spirit creature and half human, like Shining Star. Later, he came to know the mother and loved her also. He saw in the foretelling that he would lose them both. There was much pain stored up and waiting for him. He did not allow a future of extreme loneliness to halt the fulfilling of his responsibilities. He thought as he should. "Thank you for the challenge, Great Spirit. Thank you for the time I will have with her and her mother."

Prairie Blossom was a task for Shining Star. Creativity was required to teach her all she needed to know. He took her fishing to teach her the speech of various animals hidden in the underbrush. He showed her how to touch the spirits of the animals by reaching into their minds. He would take her on long walks and remind her of the conjuring spells required to accomplish what she had been born to do.

The "games" continued for four years. Prairie Blossom was now a powerful Conjurer and could protect herself.

She Who Dares knew her daughter was exceptional. She was proud of Prairie Blossom. She looked very much like She Who Dares. She had long midnight black hair, snapping black eyes, and she was slender. Her skin was not bronze though. It was creamy white, like her father's. She Who Dares thought, *I can claim that my child is more than beautiful. She is stunning.* She had no knowledge that she had given birth to a powerful Conjurer. It would have frightened her, so it was kept from her.

She Who Dares was loved and respected by her daughter. She Who Dares taught Prairie Blossom all of the Apache ways. Shining Star taught her the spiritual phenomena and the training of weapons. She had her own spear and bow. Her arrows were decorated with pink-tipped fletching. Due to the extensive lessons, Prairie Blossom had the maturity of a much older person. She knew she would need Shining Star's and She Who Dares' teachings to accomplish the foretelling. She learned their lessons well. She was not a child, even though her age was only six turns of the earth seasons. She was well prepared for the role that the Great Spirit had assigned her.

There was one important matter that she could not resolve though. She would discuss this matter with Shining Star.

Prairie Blossom talked to Shining Star late that evening. She said, "I am struggling to prepare myself for the outcome of all I have ever known. Soon, my role begins. This I know in my heart."

Shining Star said, "When the time comes and you feel as if all is lost, you must grieve, little bug. There is no other way. You must allow yourself to grieve. Grief brings us full circle. When it leaves us, we are free to clasp happiness once more. It is the way of life.

"You must always remember, all are happy in the Spirit World. We live our lives as we do, hoping to reach this wonderful place. We all pray to die with dignity and courage. Those virtues will transport us to the Spirit World."

Prairie Blossom asked, "Will you grieve, Shining Star? You are close to the Great Spirit. Can you save her?"

He said, "I will grieve very much, little bug. I think I may die of this grief. I have prayed many times to the Great Spirit for mercy. The Great Spirit's wishes will become known and cannot be changed."

Prairie Blossom said, "I feel that the time is close. When it comes, I will grieve too. Thank you, Shining Star."

Chapter Eighteen

Shining Star and She Who Dares went to their sleeping furs early. They made love in quiet tenderness. Afterward, he held her closely and fondled the smoothness of her beautiful bronze skin. He moved to her abdomen and flattened it with his palm. He noticed a slight bulge. He said, "You are getting fat, She Who Dares."

She had observed this herself. She had nurtured a hope that he would not become aware of it.

He caught her thought and felt remorseful that he had spoken without thought for her feelings. He arranged his features into a roguish expression. He grinned uninhibitedly at her. He said, "I love a woman with a little belly."

She Who Dares slapped his arm. She said, "You are unruly," conveying to him that she was not angry.

The truth was that She Who Dares did not feel better because of Shining Star's efforts at keeping peace between them. She was only twenty-three turns of the earth's seasons. She thought with petulance, *Why must I become fat?*

Shining Star heard her thoughts and vowed that he would never bring it up again. He held her closer to his body and kissed her temple. It was his prelude to lovemaking. He kissed every inch of her body and made gentle love to her.

They cried out as each reached their own satisfaction. They fell asleep with arms and legs coiled together.

* * *

She Who Dares woke from her sleep not long after the moon had risen. She could feel a gentle sensation in her abdomen. It felt like the flutter of a butterfly's wing. She had felt that once before. It was long ago. It was when she had carried Prairie Blossom in her belly. She understood then why her middle had thickened as an old woman's middle thickens with age.

She Who Dares did not think that she would ever carry Shining Star's babe. The Great Spirit had placed in her heart a lack of desire for more children. Shining Star said that she would have no more children. No, he said she would not be a mother to another child. She thought, *It means the same. Shining Star has told me that too.* Her happiness was so great. She thought with wonder, *I am carrying another babe.* She prayed, *Oh, thank you, Great Spirit. Please, as a wife, may I ask for a son to help my husband. Shining Star deserves a son, Great Spirit. Please grant my request.* She chose to wait until sunrise to divulge her secret to Shining Star.

She Who Dares did not sleep well due to her excitement. She woke much too early. She took note that it was a stunning bright and crisp winter sunrise.

Deep white snow covered the ground and the surrounding hills. She built up the fire in the hearth. She wanted Shining Star and Prairie Blossom to wake in a warm lodge.

She would prepare her husband's favorite dish to break his fast. He was fond of flat cakes with berries. She must hurry though. Firstly, she needed to pick the winterberries off the bushes growing near the frozen river. She smiled as she thought, *Shining Star will have many surprises this morning. I will take my bow and scout for small game to serve with the flat cakes.* She left without her customary cautiousness. She did not carry her bow.

She Who Dares broke through the deep snow and found the desired bushes. She examined them and found the bushes were still heavy with berries. She thought, *The birds have been generous.* She hummed as she pulled off frozen berries. Occasionally, she would spare a glance, hoping to see a nice fat rabbit. The unexpected sounds of cracking snow, sticks, and ice came from behind her. She knew the sounds were made by a very large animal. She quickly reached for her bow. She realized with a surge of terror that she had left it behind. She turned to see this animal with the courage to approach her. She saw that it was a very large puma. She Who Dares could see that there was something odd about this puma. It continued to approach her. She knew she could not kill it without her bow. She sensed as she gazed in its golden eyes that it knew it too.

She began to scream. "Shining Star, save me!"

The puma allowed her screams, as if it waited for her to tire.

Prairie Blossom ran to her first, carrying her spear.

She Who Dares screamed, "Prairie Blossom, run away!"

Prairie Blossom did not move.

She Who Dares screamed again, "Prairie Blossom, you must run! I cannot lose you."

Prairie Blossom still did not move. She continued to stare into the puma's golden eyes. She was attempting to communicate with it and to reach the puma's spirit. She was telling the puma through her mind to go away. She soon realized that the puma was a mad beast with no spirit to reach. She then knew that she must kill it with her spear.

She heard Shining Star crashing as he ran and leapt through the high snow. He was shouting, "Get back, Prairie Blossom! It is a mad creature. You cannot help her." With all of his speed and strength, Shining Star could not reach her in time. The puma sprang onto She Who Dares and took her throat out with no effort at all. It did not stop. The puma ravaged She Who Dares' throat beyond her death.

Prairie Blossom could not bear this horrible sight. She ran forward without thought. She gouged her child's spear through the eye of the puma and used all of her force to reach the puma's brain. It was an act of blatant revenge against a mad animal. Her revenge did not stop the pain of her mother's loss. Prairie Blossom could only sit by her mother and weep.

Shining Star sat beside her as he wept his heart's blood out. He felt that he had failed in his duty to protect his wife. His hoarse weeping was heartbreaking. He had known this pain would come, but he did not know of the cost to his spirit. His spirit fought to enslave itself to She Who Dares. He must fight, yet he did not wish to.

And then suddenly, a sound penetrated over their weeping. It was coming from the body of She Who Dares.

Prairie Blossom quickly lifted her mother's skirts. A very small male babe whimpered as he lay on the cold snowy ground. She picked the tiny baby up. He was perfectly formed but no bigger than the palm of your hand. Prairie Blossom handed him to Shining Star. Prairie Blossom said, "The Great Spirit has given you a son in return for all you have done for me and for what you will do for my mother. She Who Dares died with courage and with dignity."

Shining Star said, "Prairie Blossom, I loved your mother. I will build a magnificent funeral pyre to release her spirit into the Spirit World. It must be soon. Her spirit clutches at my spirit, and my spirit craves to accompany her. I must release her. I have not fulfilled my Destiny, nor have you, Prairie Blossom."

Shining Star looked at the male babe. He was very small but appeared to be healthy. He wore She Who Dares facial features. He looked closer, into his spirit. He saw that this babe would be the greatest Conjurer the Indian nation would ever know. He would also be the last one.

Shining Star did not know what this foretelling meant. He was still a young man. He would present him to the Medicine Man for naming. He would tell him what he saw in the babe's face. The Medicine Man would know.

He handed the babe back to Prairie Blossom and went back to the lodge. He grasped the handle of the sled and brought it back. He placed the puma on the sled and then She Who Dares.

Prairie Blossom asked, "Why are you taking the puma?"

He said, "This is your first kill. We must make a cape out of its hide for you."

She said, "No, I don't want to wear a cape made from the animal that killed my mother."

He said, "Your mother would want you to display this animal. Yes, it killed her, but you killed the puma. The puma hide is necessary for your Destiny. It will bring you honor. Your mother would wish it. You must see, Prairie Blossom."

She observed Shining Star and understood his heart. She sighed as an old woman who watches the antics of the young, with defeat. She must do as Shining Star says; he had always been her father.

She said, "You know best, Shining Star. I will do as you wish."

They made their way back to the lodge.

Prairie Blossom
(Fights Puma)

A woman with many talents
is worth more than gold.
—Unknown

Chapter Nineteen

The funeral pyre was built with all of Shining Star's skill and love. She Who Dares' belongings surrounded the pyre within a magical circle conjured by Shining Star. This would ensure she arrived in the Spirit World with her belongings intact.

Shining Star examined them. He saw that the works of her small hands expressed the beauty within her soul. This would bring her much honor. He held her one last time and placed She Who Dares upon the pyre. He found it very difficult to release her; her spirit was unwilling and fearful of the unknown. He felt her fear, yet he must let her go. He wept bitterly as he lay her down. He did not think he would live through this overwhelming grief, but there was the new babe to consider.

The babe was silent. It was as if he knew his mother was dead. Shining Star knew that he must do something about his hunger soon. This babe was exceptional; he was content to watch and wait.

Prairie Blossom watched Shining Star prepare for her mother's burning. She thought, *I will miss her so.*

She wept no more though. It was not from a lack of love, but from a sense of acceptance.

Prairie Blossom said, "Shining Star, I wish to use the torch. It will give me a feeling of completeness."

Shining Star said, "Are you sure, Prairie Blossom? It is a very traumatic experience."

Prairie Blossom said, "That is why I must do this, Shining Star. It will complete this part of my life. Do you understand?"

Shining Star said, "Yes, I do, Prairie Blossom. It will be as you wish. I will prepare the torch."

He finished his preparations and handed the flaming torch to Prairie Blossom. She took the torch from him and approached the pyre to sing a conjuring song with her engaging high-pitched voice. Prairie Blossom thought, *My mother is so small and vulnerable. She has her strength hidden beneath her tininess.*

Prairie Blossom's song conveyed the needed courage for She Who Dares' spirit. Prairie Blossom lit the pyre as she began to sing.

I remember the day I was born
I remember I was cradled in your arms
I remember I was given your breast to suckle
Go to the Spirit World, my dear mother
Take heart, you will never be forgotten
Pass well, my dear mother
Know that I have always loved you
You have been the best of mothers
Go to the Spirit World, my dear mother
Take heart, you will never be forgotten

THE CHOSEN ONES

You died with courage and dignity, my dear mother
The Great Spirit is proud
Let your spirit fly into the Spirit World,
do not linger in this Earthly Realm
Go to the Spirit World, my dear mother
Take heart, you will never be forgotten

Her mother's glittering white spirit rose from the flames of the pyre and ascended to the heavens.

CHAPTER TWENTY

The smoke had dissipated from She Who Dares' cremation. Her spirit had risen. She was now in the Spirit World. Her death was untimely, but dignified and brave.

Shining Star spoke to Prairie Blossom, "We must go to the Medicine Man now. We have much to learn."

Prairie Blossom said, "Yes, I see that we must go for the babe's sake alone."

Shining Star said, "Yes, I am concerned regarding the babe. He must be fed. He has been patient through the passing of the sun. He is so small. I fear he will not survive. He must have a name and be introduced to the Spirit World. Only the Medicine Man can do the proper things that protect his spirit."

Prairie Blossom said, "Yes, Shining Star. Mother would wish it done. Please wait for me." She ran into the lodge and brought the fur sling her mother had made to carry her when she was a babe. She handed it to Shining Star.

Tears came into his eyes, but did not escape. He placed the sling over his shoulders and gently laid the babe inside. He was overcome with emotion. He could see her love for this precious babe. She expressed her love in her gentle and thoughtful way, with a gift of this precious part of her past.

Shining Star said tearfully, "Thank you, Prairie Blossom. May the Great Spirit bless your Destiny and keep you safe." He would pray for this, but he could see the Great Spirit would use her talents, and her end would come. Shining Star knew that all must die sometime. It was the Black Hill's Way.

They mounted their horses and rode the wind spirits to the camp of the Black Hills Indian Tribe. Once they arrived, Shining Star rapped on the Medicine Man's door. The Medicine Man slid it open swiftly. He said, "I have been waiting. I am sorry She Who Dares met such a terrible and vicious fate. I saw Prairie Blossom conjure her spirit into the Spirit World. This is a feat not easily done in view of the fact that She Who Dares did not wish to leave. You have taught Prairie Blossom well, Shining Star."

Shining Star said, "She is a born conjurer in her own right. It was not difficult to remind her of her knowledge."

The Medicine Man said, "It is good to be modest, but I saw the time you invested in your assigned task."

Suddenly, a young woman rapped on the wall of the lodge and walked into the room. She bowed to Shining Star and to Prairie Blossom. She said, "I am called Otter. Please give me the babe. My babe died only yesterday of the white man's disease. I need to feed your son, and I wish to hold another babe."

Shining Star thrust the babe at her for feeding. She departed into an outer room to nurse this babe. She hoped to stay with this babe. She had lost her husband in the white man's wars, and she had no other kin.

Shining Star disturbed the silence. He said, "Oh Holy One, I have come for many reasons, but the most important one is the babe. He is so small. I fear he will not live. Please bestow a name upon him and make him known to the Spirit World."

The Medicine Man said, "He was born with his name. His name is Geronimo. He is known well in the Spirit World. He is the greatest Conjurer to be born and the last to be born. He will be the greatest chief the Apache Nation has ever known. As is Prairie Blossom, he is one-half Apache. He will have a good motive to choose the Apache Nation over the Black Hills Indian Tribe. He will live, Shining Star. Otter will accompany you to care for the babe."

He then spoke to Prairie Blossom. "Now, you and I will converse. I rename you Fights Puma. You did not show fear when you ran upon the puma and stabbed him through his eye and into his brain. I am sorry for you that it did not save your mother. You are a powerful Conjurer, but you could not save her against such a large mad beast. You must not carry guilt for this. You must sew your puma cape to reveal your status. You must gather your possessions and return to the Apaches. You will be seen as a Holy Woman, the first of all women to carry that title. You must leave soon. Your role is upon you. You must grasp it, and you must earn it." The Medicine Man continued, "I will not see you again, Fights Puma. I wish for you to always remain inside the Great Spirit's protection. Alas, it is not to be, but it is many turns of the earth's seasons before it occurs. I will foretell no more."

He turned and walked into an outer room.

Chapter Twenty-One

The puma skin was skinned, scraped with sharp rocks, and tanned by the hearth. Fights Puma used the tanning time to design how she would make use of the puma skin. The puma's head became a headdress. The throat became an opening to slip her head in. She sewed rawhide strips to tie it shut against the gusty winds. She took one of her pink-fletched arrows and rammed it fiercely into the puma's eye. The skin was cut large enough to accommodate her body's growth. She soon finished with this distasteful task. She slipped it over her head and gathered her belongings. They were mainly her bow, arrows, and spear. She needed nothing else.

It was time she must take leave of her adoptive father, Shining Star. She approached him with streaming tears. She said, "May the Great Spirit be with you, my father."

Shining Star felt his eyes water. He said, "May the Great Spirit be with you, my daughter."

She thought, *Oh, there is much pain in losing him.*

Shining Star said, "I have a parting gift for you. Please stay here." He brought out a huge white stallion.

Fights Puma was overwhelmed. She began to cry in earnest.

Shining Star took her in his arms and cried with her. He said, "A Holy Woman should have a pure white stallion. This is because I love you, Fights Puma. Be safe, my daughter." He turned and left as she mounted her horse.

She never saw Shining Star nor her brother again.

Chapter Twenty-Two

Fights Puma made it to the mouth of the southward trail that led to the Apache Nation before the sun's passing. She set up camp in the shady coolness on the land belonging to the adopted Black Hills Tribe. She would brave the burning, sweltering heat of the Apache trail with the sun's rising. She tied her white stallion to a tree and provided it with food and water. She touched his spirit and learned he was called Snowy. She must take care of this girl.

She drew jerky and pemmican from her pack. It was not long before she heard the crackling of sticks from her far side. She could see a large black bear. It had been a mother recently. Fights Puma could see by her large teats that she had lost her young to a meat-eating predator. She looked into the bear's eyes and could see it was not mad. It was only hungry and wanted the food she had packed.

She spoke to its spirit. "Mother, please go away. I need this food. I am going as far as the Apache Nation. I must eat on this trip."

The bear sat down on its haunches and bellowed pitifully. The bear was lonely, sad, and hungry. Fights Puma felt sympathy for her. She reached into her pack and threw pemmican to her. She said, "You must go now, Mother. You can't stay here."

The pemmican was eaten swiftly, but the bear would not leave. Fights Puma did not know what to do. She spoke to the bear again, "Please, Mother, leave me. I must sleep, and I do not wish to sleep near a hungry bear."

The bear spoke to her spirit. "It is fitting that you call me Mother. I am your grandmother, and I have been sent to watch over you while you travel. You are very special to the Great Spirit."

Fights Puma said, "Nana?"

The bear replied, "I am surprised that you still remember me. I am known as Gives Life in the Spirit World. I was renamed by the Great Spirit to show my bravery and courage. You remember me as Bright Star? I saved you. A tiny babe destined to be the first and only Holy Woman for the Apache. So, you see, I will not eat you in your sleep. Notice please, your horse is not afraid of me. I have been behind you from dawn until this sun's ending. Please, feed this bear now. It has allowed me to use its body."

Fights Puma sprinted into the trees to pick berries from the low-lying bushes. She picked as many as one bear could eat. She placed her cupped hands to the bear's muzzle so she could feed. She hurriedly brought the bear water. Fights Puma stroked her and said, "I am sorry, Mother, that you have lost your cubs."

Fights Puma could see the glistening of tears in the bear's eyes; she felt her sadness. Fights Puma touched her spirit and named her Guardian.

Fights Puma attempted to speak to Nana, but she did not respond. She was within the bear's spirit until the Apache Nation was reached.

Fights Puma slept entwined in the bear's paws. She had never felt so safe or so warm. Even the unique smell of bear was comforting. She chuckled. *Guardian must think of her smell as unique.*

The bear loped beside Fights Puma's stallion each day. They entered the Apache camp after four risings of the sun. Fights Puma entered wearing her puma cape, riding a white stallion, and followed by a black bear. Nana departed Guardian and returned to the Spirit World. The bear was not afraid of the people, and she would not leave Fights Puma.

The Apache People gathered to see. As one, they performed abeyance to her.

One spoke, "Oh, Holy Woman, we have waited so long for your appearance. Please save the Apache Nation from the greedy white man."

Fights Puma stood in her saddle and said, "I will do all I can to help the people of the Apache Nation. My spirit name is Fights Puma. I have been sent to fulfill the foretelling from the Great Spirit.

"In many turnings of the sun, there will be another who will come. He is much greater than I. His name is Geronimo. He is the greatest Conjurer to ever be born and the last to be born. Apache people, believe. You must wait for Geronimo. He is yet a babe, but his power is immense. He will be young when he arrives. He will be a great fighter. He will sting the white man. He will be the greatest chief ever known to the Apache people."

The people were excited and murmured beneath their hands at this foretelling. The Braves made war cries and war dances out of excitement. There would be real fighting against the white man. The Apache would get their lands back. They began to chant loudly and hopefully, "Geronimo, Geronimo, Geronimo."

Somewhere far away, a babe began to stir restlessly. He wished to answer their call.

Fights Puma thought, *A small part of my mission is complete*. She had prepared the Apache people for the arrival of Geronimo. This would not be forgotten by the people. It would be discussed over many campfires for many turnings of the sun.

Fights Puma did not know that Geronimo must come, as he would be lured by her murder. Yes, he must come in order to avenge his sister's death and then take his place among the Apache tribe.

Fights Puma staggered. She supported herself by grasping her saddle horn. The trip had been hot and grueling. She had not eaten much food. She had shared evenly with Guardian. She spoke to the Apache people, "I would like to rest after my journey. Where may I lie?"

The Medicine Man spoke, "Holy Woman, we have prepared a lodge for you. You will find it very comfortable. The horse and the bear are attached to the south end of your lodge. Would you prefer that the bear remain with you?"

Fights Puma said, "The bear will not be penned. She will be with me at all times. Her name is Guardian. She is a spirit bear."

The people brought them food and water and cared for Snowy. Once they had their meal, Fights Puma and Guardian slept until moonrise. They woke refreshed.

Chapter Twenty-Three

Fights Puma was called to duty. Guardian accompanied her as always. It was necessary to speak to the Medicine Man. She heard his calls to her spirit while she slept. He needed to speak to her urgently. She wore her puma cape to display her status. She was escorted to his lodge by two Braves even though she remembered the way as a babe. Tears stung her eyes. The memory of her mother facing the tribunal came to the forefront of her mind. She could see now that it was necessary if Geronimo was to be born. She could see further now into the Great Spirit's purpose.

She wished her mother had not died. She was not fated to die; it was because she met the mad puma. She knew that her mother's death was not purposed by the Great Spirit. Bringing Geronimo forth was the purpose of the Great Spirit. He saved Geronimo from the puma and kept the tiny babe alive for hours. Geronimo is a creation of the Great Spirit. Geronimo had a large obligation.

Fights Puma cleared her mind. They were nearly at the Medicine Man's lodge. She wondered what she could tell him; no doubt, he would ask her the appropriate questions. He would find out what he needed to know.

The Medicine Man asked many questions. They were for the sake and health of the tribe. Fights Puma understood that this was his role as Medicine Man.

He asked, "Why did you come here?"

She answered, "The Great Spirit sent me."

He asked, "Why did he send you here?"

She answered, "The Great Spirit will make my role known."

He said, "I am glad you are here for the Great Spirit's purposes, but you are a child."

She said, "Don't you know me, Medicine Man?"

He said, "No, your conjuring powers have blocked my sight."

She said, "I was Prairie Blossom. Now I am Fights Puma."

He said, "Are you the Conjurer that sang She Who Dares into the Spirit World? This powerful act was seen and heard by all Holy Men."

Her eyes moistened as she spoke, "I am the one."

He asked no more questions.

Chapter Twenty-Four

Fights Puma brooded. She spoke, "I have been with the Apache Tribe for several weeks. The people have come to know us. There has been no fighting among the whites and the people. I know my status is a Holy Woman, but what is my role? I cannot cure the sick or feed the hungry. My every need is anticipated and fulfilled. I have given nothing in return. I know it should not be this way. I should be helping the people in some way. I feel useless."

Suddenly, the sounds of a battle taking place came to her ears. She opened the door to her lodge and felt horror flood through her body. There were wounded men lying on the ground moaning, the sounds of terrified women screaming, the slapping of bare feet running for safety, and crying children, lost or forgotten by their parents. She prayed, "Oh, Great Spirit, please guide me."

Fights Puma came out of her lodge. She grasped that her role demanded she stop this battle. She walked to the mouth of the trail that led into the Apache village. Guardian shielded her with her huge black body. The Braves followed behind them, begging her to go back to the lodge where she would be safe. They could not force her. They did not dare lay their hands on a Holy Woman. The consequences were death with no life in the Spirit World.

She ordered them, "Braves, go back to safety. I am a powerful Conjurer. I have Guardian to shield me."

They said, "Holy Woman, we will not obey a command that puts you in danger." They formed a circle around her and allowed the bear to lead the way.

Rifles were blasting from the base of the trail. She conjured a shield that encompassed the entire top of the trail. It appeared to the whites as if she arrogantly presented herself as a target for their rifles. She calmly stood and examined the whites. They were crawling along the trail; it was strewn with boulders. They were using the boulders as shields to evade the arrows shot by the Braves. The arrows lay haphazardly throughout the trail.

Fights Puma stood and considered for a tense moment. She asked herself quietly, "What do I do now?"

The answer was sent to her from the Great Spirit. "You must ask them why they are shooting at you. You must parley with them."

Fights Puma spoke in a deafening, conjured voice as she stood beside Guardian. "Why are you shooting at us?"

Her voice echoed throughout the countryside and drowned out the sound of rifles shooting.

One man looked intensely at her. He was an older man. He was sinewy and lanky. He wore a battered old hat encircled with a shedding snakeskin band. He had one good eye and a black hole where his other eye belonged. It appeared to Fights Puma that he was the chief of these scraggly men. He was in the fore. She brought her gaze to him.

This action brought his gaze to her from his clear light eye. She felt like a moth drawn to a flame. She could see plainly that his spirit was mad. She could feel in her spirit that her death would come from his hand. She shivered in the hot Texas heat. She commanded herself to have courage. She must talk to this mad creature. The Great Spirit directed her to ask a small question. She could not disobey.

He halted the firing of rifles by the simple act of raising his arm. He shouted up the trail to Fights Puma, "You are the Holy Woman we have heard about. I see your bear and your puma cape. We have heard of your powers. We seek one thing and one thing only. If you will give it to us, we will leave peacefully."

Fights Puma said, "What is it you seek, brother? What are you called?"

He was taken aback by her politeness. He said, "I am called Butch. I seek the Injun squaw called Coyote Hunter. She killed her white husband. This hat is all that is left of him." He held the hat in the air for her to see. "I know you Injuns know where she is. It is only right she pay for her crime, Holy Woman."

Fights Puma said, "When did this happen, Butch?"

Butch said, "It has been years back, but I can still smell her stink. I know she is near."

Fights Puma said, "I will tell you the truth, Butch. You must end this hunt. I tell you upon my honor, Coyote Hunter was laid on her funeral pyre two moons ago." She sealed her fate as she said, "Coyote Hunter was my mother, Butch. This puma skin I wear took her life by ripping out her throat. I killed the puma out of revenge. I wear its skin. You must see the truth, Butch. She is in the Spirit World and cannot be found by anyone. I lit her funeral pyre. I sang her into the Spirit World."

Fights Puma wished to give him an understanding that would reach beyond his madness. She failed to remember that you cannot reason with a mad creature. She only felt blood calling to blood. He was her father's brother. He was her uncle.

She continued, "Coyote Hunter was punished by the Apache Nation. She was exiled with a babe. That babe was me, Butch. We lived in the Black Hills until her death. She is gone, Butch. Let this be over."

Fights Puma did not reach him in spite of her efforts. She had given him every chance to overcome his madness.

Butch became angry at her words. Out of frustration, he threw the ragged hat on the ground and spit toward Fights Puma. He screamed, "You are just another lying Injun squaw! She lives, I feel it in my guts. I will find her."

His men stalked off, muttering loudly. "I told you the bastard was crazy. We have been wasting our time looking for a dead squaw."

Butch bellowed, "Come back, men! I am right, I tell you. She is here, I feel it. You know what Coyote Hunter did to poor Mitch. He wouldn't have hurt a fly. She left her husband for the animals to eat. She deserves the same medicine." He spun around to face Fights Puma. He spoke in a menacing tone of voice, "Since you are her kid, you need to die for her crimes."

Fights Puma could see the death wish in his eye. She also could see his cunning. Shining Star had taught her that madness in spirit takes many faces. She shivered again. Guardian stood up and bellowed threateningly. The Braves jumped in front of her, arrows drawn.

Fights Puma showed her power by casting her voice out loudly, "Think! Uncle Butch. It is not wise to threaten a Conjurer. I have told you what happened to Coyote Hunter. Yet I cannot convince you. You have become a mad beast deep in your spirit. This puma allowed its spirit to become mad. Go away, Uncle Butch, and do not come back. If you do, you are fated to die like my father, Mitch. I tell you as a Conjurer, your feet will not walk this trail again, and I have told you what will happen if you do."

She turned her back on him and walked into her lodge. The Braves shot arrows to cover her retreat. Guardian walked behind her, using her body as a shield.

Once she reached the inside of her lodge, Fights Puma shivered violently. She had never been the object of such hatred. Guardian stood, wrapped her paws around her, and held her tightly. Fights Puma wished she could communicate.

Guardian said to her spirit, "I have been here all along."

Fights Puma was not surprised. She spoke solemnly, "I see my death in the way he looks at me, Guardian. He is my uncle, and he is mad. He will kill kin."

Guardian said, "Please watch the one-eyed white man. His spirit wishes to harm you. You must take care. Do not think of him as kin. He is a mad spirit only. You are not ill-fated, Fights Puma. You must realize, life consists of one possibility or of many. The Great Spirit decides for all creatures according to his purpose. This spirit creature has been sent to guard you. You must make this trouble-free for me."

Fights Puma smiled and hugged Guardian. "I will. I know my role now, Guardian."

Guardian asked, "What is your role, little one?"

Fights Puma said, "My role is to keep the fighting between the whites and the Apaches as nonexistent as possible. I am to be the peacemaker until Geronimo comes."

Guardian said, "That is right, little one. A Holy Woman can complete this destiny. All women desire peace."

Chapter Twenty-Five

Fights Puma had seen twenty-six summers. She had grown into a beautiful woman. She looked as her mother had, with two exceptions. Her skin color was not bronze, and her hair color was distinctive. There were dominant silver streaks laced among an abundance of midnight black hair.

Guardian explained, "The silver in your hair characterizes wisdom of a Conjurer. The day will come when all of your hair is silver."

Fights Puma asked, "Guardian, my friend, is it time for Geronimo's arrival? I weary of the constant parley with the white man. He tries to take more and more of Apache land. Geronimo will shoo these whites away like bothersome flies."

Guardian said, "Not yet, my precious one. Please do not wish for his coming. His face, you will not see."

Fights Puma said spiritedly, "What do you mean, Guardian? He is my brother. Of course, I will see his face. I will see Geronimo as soon as he arrives."

Guardian said, "More, I cannot say. The Great Spirit has placed restrictions on me. I can tell you that there will be great pain followed by great happiness. All creatures will become what they wish to be in the end. It will be the same with you."

Fights Puma said, "That is good to hear. I have been sad and spent these last few moons."

Guardian said, "Your feelings are destined to be. They will pass soon, love. I also weary of the white man's demands. Fights Puma, you have not forgotten the mad one, have you? It is important that you always keep him in mind. This poor mad creature is a danger to you."

Fights Puma said, "Yes, Guardian, I think of him often and wish I could heal his madness with my conjuring powers. It would be good to have an uncle."

Guardian said in alarm, "Please do not think that way. He is mad and cannot be healed. You must not pity him or feel sorrow for him. It will be understood as weakness if you should encounter him. Please do not close your ears to me, Fights Puma. Please hear me, my precious one. Pity and sorrow would result in an unearned death for you. Promise me that you will flee from him. Your conjuring powers have no effect on a mad soul. You know this to be true. You wear the puma hide as proof. You must escape him."

Fights Puma said heatedly, "Yet I killed this puma, Guardian. I promise you, I will wear my bow for protection."

Guardian said, "Please listen, my precious one. Flee him! Do not fight him. Hide from his madness."

Fights Puma said peevishly, "Hush, Guardian, it is enough. I will not run like a rabbit from a madman. Enough has been said."

With these words, Guardian perceived the end of Fights Puma's life. She would choose to fight, and she would die. She would die a death of honor and dignity. She would be welcomed into the Spirit World.

Guardian would grieve her absence. She had grown fond of her, but there would be another coming soon.

Chapter Twenty-Six

Fights Puma knew in her heart that she had behaved rebelliously. She had portrayed herself as a young resentful child. She asked herself, "How could I treat Guardian so callously? She has done so much for me. I believe it is because of the restless feelings that plague me from the sun's rising till the moon's rising. I feel a new circumstance approaching, but my conjuring powers have not allowed me to see. I do not sleep. There is blackness in my dreams. It is worrying to me."

She put her thoughts behind her for the moment. She must care for the people. Many of them were falling ill of the white man's disease. Fights Puma knew their only hope was the Medicine Man, his potions, and his spells. She could have sent a Brave to fetch him, but she wanted a change of scenery. She chose to walk even though the Medicine Man's lodge lay far away. It would take her many footsteps to arrive. He would know she was coming.

As Fights Puma made her arrangements to depart, she ordered her guards and Guardian to stay. She would remain on Apache land. She would be safe. She did not need an escort. Guardian refused to obey this command. The guards did not dare refuse. They bowed their heads in acknowledgment.

Fights Puma was cross with Guardian. She concluded it was best to allow Guardian to come along. She knew that Guardian would follow her if she did not allow her to come. Guardian was given the task to guard Fights Puma from the Great Spirit. She would not be thwarted, no matter how Fights Puma felt.

Fights Puma thought, *Oh, it is so good to be alive on this earth. All of the beauty surrounding me belongs to the Great Spirit.*

Fights Puma could see the cold season approaching rapidly. She read the many signs hidden in the behavior of the animals, trees, and birds. It was an ending to the warm plentiful season. She could feel cooler air. She saw colorful leaves lying on the ground. Her feet trod upon them; they were not yet dry and brittle. She thought, *Yes, it is so. The cold season of hunger is approaching. The Great Spirit does not vary his ways.*

Fights Puma was beginning to feel her heart fill with happiness. She knew she would not feel her best until she apologized to Guardian. Fights Puma thought, *I will begin my apology and make this a perfect time for us both.*

Guardian heard her thought. "It is all right, love. You are only facing many problems with the whites and with the spirits that come with womanhood."

Fights Puma said, "Dearest Guardian, I am so sorry for my behavior. I should have listened to your wisdom. You must be ancient. I have known you and your counsel since the turnings of the sun that ended my childhood."

Guardian said, "Yes, dear one, I am ancient in comparison to you." She chuckled. "Please walk a bit slower for this ancient black bear."

They walked farther and came upon bushes sagging heavily with ripe berries. They thanked the Great Spirit for this bounty before they stopped to eat. The berries were juicy and the sweetest Fights Puma had ever tasted. She stuffed so many berries in her mouth. Juice ran down her chin.

Guardian laughed at this sight and said, "Fights Puma, I thought you left your childhood behind you."

Fights Puma responded, "Not now. I want to be a child for one more sunrise to moonrise. Aren't these berries good?"

Guardian said, "Yes, they are the best I have ever tasted, Fights Puma. I would do the same if I could."

Fights Puma picked a large handful and thrust them into Guardian's mouth. Soon, there was juice running from Guardian's mouth. Fights Puma laughed as Guardian ate them.

Fights Puma thought, *It is so beautiful. I am so happy that Guardian and I are having such a good time. It has been many moons since I have felt so carefree. This sun's rising has been an auspicious sign. It reminds me of my birth. I feel there is something new awaiting me. This is a morning of celebration. I have only begun to feel and see the beauty of the earth surrounding me. I have only begun to enjoy the delightful company of Guardian. My conjuring powers foretell there is something rewarding for Guardian and myself. There is blackness to pass through before the goodness becomes apparent. Guardian and I must have courage to overcome this blackness. Guardian is a spirit creature. She will have bravery. I will emulate her. I have much to learn.* Fights Puma said, "Thank you for the foretelling, Great Spirit. I will display courage."

She heard a loud cracking noise coming from nearby and recognized the sound of a rifle shot.

Guardian fell to the ground and rolled onto her side. Fights Puma heard her last wailing thought: *I have been so wrong!*

Fights Puma tugged on Guardian. She knew she was gone, but Fights Puma did not wish to believe. She was crying out, "Get up, Guardian! Get up now! Get up!" Guardian did not get up. Fights Puma thought to arm herself with bow and arrow. She was peering into the woods, looking for her target. She did not see him, but she heard him clearly.

He said, "I told you I would get you, Coyote Hunter. You killed my brother, Mitch. You left him for the wild animals to eat. I am going to leave you and your bear for the wild animals. I figured if I waited long enough, you would come along. Yep, I am going to kill you, Coyote Hunter. Begging me to live won't do any good. Ain't no woman tricks will get to me either. Mitch always had a soft heart for a woman, but I never cared much for them. Do you want to cry? Beg me for your life? I might be feeling generous, or I might not. There's only one way to find out, Coyote Hunter."

Fights Puma conjured as he talked. She thought to reach his mind. She saw nothing but blackness. There was no humanity in his spirit. There was only confusion, blackness, and madness. This helped her to recognize him as her uncle, even though she could not see him.

She understood that this man was the blackness of her dreams. The dreams caused her to wake up suffocating. This was the blackness made known to her, the madness of her uncle.

The Great Spirit communicated to her an image of courage and indicated happiness once this hardship was over.

Her conjuring powers had revealed long ago that she would die by Butch's hand. She knew she was going to die very soon.

She remembered the things Guardian told her. Flee. Guardian had told her to flee the madness.

She had said with false courage, "I will not flee like a rabbit from a madman."

She remembered Guardian's last forlorn words: "I have been so wrong."

She made her choice. She squared her shoulders and laid her hand on her heart. She said, "Please do not miss, Uncle Butch."

Her last moments, her last thoughts, and her last words were relayed to all Indian Conjurers.

Geronimo comes!

GREAT CHIEF GERONIMO

Be wary when leaving your mark
upon the world,
it is rarely achieved without leaving a dramatic scar.
—Unknown

Chapter Twenty-Seven

The Medicine Man heard Fights Puma's last call to all conjurers. He ran to her side, carrying only his bow and arrows. He knew he could not save her life. He could foresee that she was awaiting the Spirit World. She was beyond any physical pain.

His deference urged him to run faster. It was vital that her holy body be respected and not disfigured. At last he reached Fights Puma and the bear. The madman was sharpening his hunting knife and talking to Fights Puma's bloody body. The Medicine Man took a moment to listen to his babbling. The madman spoke of her as Coyote Hunter. His madness did not allow him to notice the Medicine Man or the Braves running from the camp.

The Medicine Man raised his bow. He shot the madman in the right shoulder. He screamed in pain and dropped the knife. His arm was now useless. The Medicine Man said, "I wish to kill you for this, madness or not. This privilege belongs to Geronimo. You will face his wrath for this deed. He will kill you with no empathy. Geronimo will come soon, you will see."

Butch asked with belligerence, "Who in hell is this Injun called Geronimo?"

The Medicine Man said, "You will see soon enough, crazy white man. No, I will tell you. He is Fights Puma's brother. She is our Holy Woman you have killed out of your madness. She is not Coyote Hunter."

The madman cackled. "I ain't scared to die by no Injun's hand. I only lived to kill Coyote Hunter."

The Medicine Man said, "You will be very afraid and very soon. Braves, take him away, if you must drag him. Lock him in a lodge and place guards on him. Please bring sleds. Fights Puma and the bear must be taken back to camp. I will wait here and protect their bodies."

As the Medicine Man waited, all Indian Conjurers began to hear the faint sound of hoofbeats in their minds. The hoofbeats were traveling at a very rapid pace. Geronimo was riding the wind spirits. The Medicine Man thought, *He will be here quickly.*

The Medicine Man saw that he must speak with Great Chief, Eagle Heart. His role was foretold long ago by the Great Spirit. Geronimo will be the Great Chief. It is spoken of in the ancient prophecies. It is foreordained. Geronimo will be called the greatest chief the Apache Nation will ever know. He will define the Indian.

THE CHOSEN ONES

The Medicine Man departed when the sleds arrived. He felt an urgency to speak with Chief Eagle Heart, who was preparing to leave the lodge that had been built especially for a Great Chief. He too could hear the hoofbeats in his mind. He knew the ancient prophecies as well.

Eagle Heart thought, *Geronimo is coming. He is young, and all know the young are blind. He is coming, and he is bringing hate and rage in his heart and into the hearts of the people.*

Eagle Heart knew this to be true. He had meditated on many ancient prophecies. There would be much warfare and much death while Geronimo was chief. Eagle Heart had kept this knowledge to himself. It would be misunderstood. The people would think he did not wish to step down. Eagle Heart did not understand why these cruel things must happen, but he was a lowly man. He had been given enough good things in his long life. Eagle Heart would walk; there would not be even a horse for this old man. He would settle in a peaceful place. It would be best that way. He grieved for the people as they would suffer. He knew they would learn to suffer gladly as long as the whites suffered too. He prayed, "Oh, Great Spirit, why must these terrible things occur? Have your people angered you? I beg of you to soften Geronimo's heart."

The Medicine Man rapped urgently on the old chief's door. He said, "Eagle Heart, you are packed. I came to assist you. I knew you would wish to be gone soon after Geronimo arrives. I will miss you, my friend. Tell me, do you hear the hoofbeats?"

Chief Eagle Heart said, "Yes, I hear them. He is riding the wind spirits and will be here soon. I will speak and make a formal declination for the people. I must present the headdress, tunic, and leggings of a Great Chief to Geronimo. I will leave after this ceremony takes place. I will miss you also, my friend. Take care."

The Medicine Man said, "I would go with you. I have studied the ancient prophecies too. I know what will happen. It will begin with the madman's death, and the cruelty within Geronimo will spread to the white man. I cannot leave the people without any guidance. You must leave. You cannot cross Geronimo."

Eagle Heart said, "Yes, that is why I am leaving. There cannot be more than one Great Chief."

Chapter Twenty-Eight

The sound of the hoofbeats became deafening in the minds of the Conjurers. They were powerful men, but filled with fear. They perceived that Geronimo's arrival would change their lives. His coming was foretold long ago.

The Braves saw that all was prepared. The funeral pyre was built grandly. Fights Puma was lying beside her loyal black bear, Guardian. They remained together in life and together in death. It was believed that Fights Puma, a woman of known courage, would escort the faithful bear into the Spirit World.

The Conjurers soon began to hear genuine hoofbeats, much louder and much closer.

The madman began to scream. He had reason to fear his fate. Geronimo had reached through his mad mind and given him a foreknowing of his death. The people whispered behind their hands, "It is a sign. Geronimo is coming."

The hoofbeats drew closer very quickly. A foaming overpowered black stallion galloped into the camp. Geronimo was clinging to him using his knees and grasping the stallion's black mane. The people gazed at him with unhidden admiration; they had as one accepted him on sight as the Great Chief who was revealed in the ancient prophecies. His conjuring power was overwhelming; all could feel the impact of his emotional distress.

He was only a youth by the turnings of the sun, yet his face was set with the grief and rage of a man. His long straight black hair streamed behind him. He wore tanned riding leathers, beaded and stained with conjurer's symbols. He resembled his mother, She Who Dares. He was long in body. His nose was strong and hooked like the eagle's beak. His lips were full and sensual. His eyes were snapping black like his ancestors. His skin was as bronze as the metal the white man wrought. His features had their place with the Apaches.

The madman continued to scream.

Geronimo leapt off the horse's back. It continued to gallop through the camp. Geronimo allowed no time for greetings. He followed the screams of the madman to the lodge where he was imprisoned. He burst the door open using his conjuring power. He grasped him roughly and forced the madman out of the lodge so all could witness his punishment.

Geronimo spoke loudly. "You do not fear this Injun, white man? That is what you said. Your screams give lie to your lack of fear. You have killed my sister.

I will avenge her death. I will kill you with less mercy than you showed her."

The madman could not answer; he could only scream.

Geronimo conjured a spell and chanted. He spoke again, "Look at my face."

The madman did not stop screaming, and he did not uncover his useful eye with his palm.

Geronimo spoke, "You choose not to bring your eye to my face? You must know, I will allow you no free will. It is only what you gave my dear sister."

Geronimo began to chant.

The madman's hand moved against his will toward his face. He stared at Geronimo, pleading for compassion. It was evident in his gaze. However, his pleading had no effect on Geronimo.

The people began to feel uneasy. The madman had no chance. He could not fight Geronimo's conjuring. The people realized that Fights Puma was highly respected; they would not interfere or avert their eyes. It would show disrespect. They realized that this was Geronimo's revenge against the madman who killed his sister. Their fear of Geronimo's rage was evident. They were also fearful of his conjuring abilities. It was beyond belief that Geronimo had reached the mind of a madman. This was unheard of among Apache conjurers. His power was truly fear-inspiring. All the people from all tribes knew what was foretold: Geronimo would be the most powerful of the Conjurers and the last of the Conjurers.

Geronimo continued to chant. The madman was forced to insert his finger into his only eye. His finger then crooked, and he pulled out his own eye. Geronimo continued to chant until the madman held his eye out toward him. Geronimo knocked his eye onto the ground and spat.

The madman ceased screaming and began weeping. There were no tears, just ragged sobs.

Geronimo spoke, "You are blind, white man. Do you wish to live?"

The madman consented by moving his head.

Geronimo thought, *He has no courage. He would live as a blind man rather than face a brave and dignified death.* Geronimo felt disgust for this madman. It came into his heart to kill him painfully to avenge his sister. His grief was not through with him.

He felt his sister's spirit brush against his own. She allowed her feelings to enter Geronimo briefly. She did not wish suffering on the madman. Geronimo respected her feelings, but there was no question that the madman must die. He simply closed the breath of Life, ceasing its entry into the mad creature.

He was dead soon. It came to pass as his dear sister had wished.

Once he brought an end to the madman, Geronimo proceeded onward to see Fights Puma. He sprinted to the funeral pyre. He saw her cape of puma hide. He examined her face to see that it had not been marred.

He spoke aloud, "It is her. This is my dear sister. She is beautiful. It is fitting she is placed with her dear companion. I did not know my dear sister, yet she is one that I have loved."

The Medicine Man stepped forward and spoke. "Each of them died with courage, dignity, and honor."

Geronimo said, "I know of this. I saw their deaths. Dear sister called me as she died. I must light her pyre and guide her into the Spirit World. She is still waiting. She is fearful. This must be done without delay."

The Braves provided lit torches. Geronimo began to light the pyre. He had fashioned a conjuring rhyme designed to give her courage. All knew her spirit could not remain in the earthly realm; it must ascend to the Spirit World. He spoke loudly, calling to Fights Puma.

I remember dawn stars, beneath their light I was born,
My birth came by expulsion; I was alone and forlorn.
I remember lying on the cold winter snow,
I saw I must cry, or I would die from the cold.
I remember you laid me in my father's arms,
His pride was apparent; I was saved from all harm.
I remember you swathed me in your fur sling,
I was then sheltered from winter's sting.
I remember you loved me as time eased your grief,
In spite of your loss, you were selfless with me.
I remember the sight of your eyes shining bright,
I could see that your spirit was light.
I cried as a babe, I foresaw I would lose,
I was certain in my heart, I would never know you.
Do not be ruled by fear, my dear sister
Your spirit shall return to He who gives it.

A great white eagle, wings outstretched, ascended from the burning pyre. It bore a black bear cub in its strong talons as it flew to the Spirit World.

Chapter Twenty-Nine

*F*ights Puma's spirit had flown. Geronimo thought, *It was touching. She was born a human infant with strong conjuring abilities. She left the earthly realm as a pure white eagle bearing a beloved black cub. I can see only a full-grown mature eagle could fly while carrying a bear cub. Fights Puma would not leave her faithful bear in this earthly realm to wander alone. Her spirit chose well.*

Tears filled Geronimo's eyes; they were not tears of grief. The tears arose from the feeling of pride in his sister's accomplishments. Dear Sister held back the whites from Apache lands for many turnings of the sun. She had proved to be a special woman.

Fights Puma was the only woman Geronimo had loved. He craved to know her many times, his only sister. All he had of her was his memories as a small babe. He should be grateful; they were beloved. The Great Spirit had chosen otherwise for Fights Puma and himself. Geronimo did not regret this. The Great Spirit knew best.

The madman was dragged out of the village by his feet and onto the trail. Geronimo meant to see he would be eaten by wild animals. Geronimo thought, *Butch is a gory sight to be seen.* He was stripped of his clothes, his face was covered in blood, and his eye was stuck to his breastbone. His ragged old hat was shoved down, tightly placed on his head. *I wish for him to be recognized by the whites. I mean for the body of Uncle Butch to be a warning to the whites. I want them to see what will happen if another of their race kills an Apache. I can see that all is as I have ordered. The Braves have done well.*

Geronimo did not think of the rage this would breed among the whites. Butch was a well-known character. They saw it this way; old Butch's death was cruelty, pure and simple. Killing him was one thing; it was well deserved for the killing of Fights Puma. Torturing him before killing him was not accepted by the whites. Butch was obviously mad. Why was this not considered by this new chief Geronimo? They could only hope it was because Fights Puma was his sister. The whites feared this may lead to worse acts from the Apache. It was true that neither side understood the other. It was evident that Fights Puma was gone now.

Old Chief Eagle Heart chose to step down. The foretelling demanded he did so. He had remained obedient to prophecy throughout his life. He hastily met with Geronimo and presented him with the items bestowed on a new Apache chief. He left the camp immediately after presenting the beautiful headdress, tunic, leggings, and the bow with eagle feather–fletched arrows. He thought as he spoke with Geronimo, *I am fearful. I may not control my tongue, and I will chastise Geronimo for the treatment of the madman. I know it would mean my death if I spoke out. It is true. It is expected by the people that the old chief be devoured by the young chief. That is as it should be. An old chief can live out his usefulness. I also know I cannot win against Geronimo's conjuring powers. I must let it pass. The people are with Geronimo. They will never respect me again as chief. I will not deny my destiny. I will step down and leave as an exile must do. The Great Spirit will see that I will be rewarded for my obedience and my conduct in bowing to the foretelling. I will live out my days in peace.*

Geronimo felt a deep sadness at old Chief Eagle Heart's departure. He thought, *It is sad to see that all people come to uselessness following many turns of the sun. Old Eagle Heart has outlived his usefulness. If I am not killed in battle, there will come a reckoning for the passing of my prime. I feel despair. I remember his bowed shoulders as he walked slowly away. His bundle was small for one with so many years of standing as an Apache Great Chief. I will remember his grief alongside his obedience to the foretelling. It is truth. All people must live the destiny the Great Spirit has chosen.*

Chapter Thirty

A moon had passed since Fights Puma's spirit had flown. Geronimo had been recognized as the Great Chief by the people. He made a beginning by having frequent powwows with the Warrior Braves. He spoke persuasively to their spirits. He did not like the whites' intrusion on Apache land. Geronimo wanted all Apache land returned by the Great White Chief in Washington, DC. He wanted the buffalo herds returned to the Indian tribes. The Indians depended on the yearly return of the buffalo herds to survive. The whites killed and wasted the buffalos' meat; they took the choicest parts and left the rest to rot. It was an offense to the Indian. The Indians believed you must respect the spirit of all living creatures. It is good to hunt if you are hungry, but the Great Spirit demands that you thank the fallen buffalo for the bounty of his body. This wanton waste by the whites was not respectful. The whites killed when they were not hungry. That was not the Apache way. The buffalo herds traveled in amounts much larger than an Indian could see standing upon a tall rock. Now, there were very little buffalo left for the Indian.

The whites were afraid. The way of Old Butch's death caused them to be full of fear and anger against Geronimo. Out of their fear, they began to plot against him. They hoped for the death of this new Great Chief. They placed hidden scouts along the trail with orders to kill on sight.

The plot was doomed to failure. Geronimo was a great conjurer; he sensed the scouts, knew their motives, and scented the metal of the rifles. He was pleased regarding the assignation attempt. This gave him good reason to attack the whites. He would attack their settlements and gallop back to safety before they could take action. He would destroy outlying farms with flaming arrows. He would poison their wells. He would trample their crops. He would steal their horses, their women, and their children. This would be the beginning of a long war.

Geronimo felt in his heart that he was following the Great Spirit's intentions. He was sure the Great Spirit would push him onward if he should falter.

Chapter Thirty-One

Geronimo did all the terrible things he said he would do. He grew to be an old man, and he continued to fight the whites. The Great White Chief sent the US Army to capture Geronimo. They were a very large force of fighting men. Geronimo's conjuring was of no use against such a force of men.

He was ambushed while herding buffalo to the edge of a mesa to feed his people. The whites came from the bushes, the rocks, and the scraggly trees. He could not run, nor could he go back; his only choice was arrest. He knew in his heart that he would not be forgiven for all the things he had done to the whites. He was sure they would torture him and his Braves. He determined that the whites were not going to steal the buffalo that he and his Braves had herded. This choice was the undoing of Geronimo.

He commanded his Braves, "Panic the buffalo and cause them to run off the mesa to their deaths. If you love me, you will follow the buffalo without fear. Call my name as you fall. The Great Spirit will hear, and you will be taken to the Spirit World. This I promise you."

The Braves began to chant loudly, "Geronimo, Geronimo, who is the Greatest of Chiefs." They began to move the buffalo to the highest edge of the mesa.

A white soldier was watching. He was overwhelmed. He yelled to the Great White Chief, "The crazy Injun is going to do it! He is going to ride off the mesa."

Geronimo shouted, "Braves, stampede the buffalo! You and your horses must run. I will follow you."

The herd of buffalo ran over the highest edge of the mesa. The Braves were off the mesa and in the air. They were upright on their horses and crying out the name of Geronimo. Geronimo turned his head at a full gallop and waved his hand to the Great White Chief.

He looked at the end of the mesa he was approaching and called out, "Great Spirit, please bring your faithful warriors into the Spirit World!" He was over the edge of the mesa before he finished his prayer.

He sent his last words to the women in camp. "We are caught by the whites. Our spirits are free."

The women grieved, each in their own way. They prayed for the spirits of their men. It was all a woman could do.

Chapter Thirty-Two

Geronimo was falling through the air; he felt a sensation of lightness. He reached for his conjuring powers reflexively in order to slow his downward fall. He realized that his powers were lost to him. He could not stop this horrible act he had committed. He had chosen, out of reckless pride, to gallop off the enormous mesa. His horse had dislodged him at the brink of the mesa in order to save itself. He was thrown over the horse's head and off the mesa.

He was ending his own life rather than lose this battle and come to terms with the Great White Chief's punishment. He tilted his head upward and prayed silently and quickly for forgiveness. "Oh Great Spirit, I do ask myself why I have done this terrible thing? I see that I have been defiant, prideful, and thoughtless. I have behaved as if my life meant nothing, my precious life, given to me from you. Dear Great Spirit, I beg of you, my Braves simply obeyed my command. Please allow them to enter the Spirit World. I am responsible for their deaths."

He saw that his downward fall was all but concluded. He shouted aloud, using the last breath that would ever enter his lungs, "Oh Great Spirit, you have guarded and blessed me all of my life. Please extend your mercy and forgiveness to my spirit and allow me to enter the Spirit World!"

There was no pain; there was merely complete blackness as he struck the tremendous jagged boulder. His wisdom, his courage, his memories, and his pride were gone. His body was bruised and torn nearly apart. He was now a shell of the great living man he had been.

The Great White Chief watched Geronimo's fall. He was saddened by the loss of such a great warrior, one who had the courage to escape his trap, even though it meant his life. He said a silent prayer for Geronimo's spirit to the god that belonged to the white man; he requested unconditional forgiveness.

The Great Spirit responded to this heartfelt prayer even though the Great White Chief spoke in silence to his own god. His prayer was spoken with such grief and respect on behalf of a great warrior. The Great Spirit chose to allow the Great White Chief to observe that his mercy was great and given to all his creatures.

A great white eagle swooped down from the heights through the darkening purple sky. From legend, the Great White Chief knew this majestic eagle to be Fights Puma, Geronimo's half-sister. Her talons were strong and spread far apart. She gave him the impression that she could not hesitate nor allow Geronimo's precious body to lie longer than necessary. In her loving heart, she must fly using all the speed that she was capable of and grasp with all gentleness her half-brother, Geronimo.

She lifted her burden tenderly and soared away, far beyond the Great White Chief's sight. Many lifelike shadows glided through the darkening sky behind her. The Great White Chief was privileged to see her bear Geronimo's shattered, much loved, and holy body with faith and reverence to the forgiving and loving bosom of the Great Spirit.

THE ANCIENT ONE

(GILDED ROSE)

The tragedy of life is not death,
but what we let die in us as we live.
—Unknown

Chapter Thirty-Three

The abandoned Apache women were bewildered and ashamed. Their Braves had taken their own lives rather than face the ambush carefully prepared by the Great White Chief. The women knew it was not the Apache way to display such cowardice. Apaches do not fear punishment or death by the white man's hand in battle. The Apache way demanded that they fight bravely, even while awaiting the end of their lives.

Even so, the women prayed for their Braves' spirits. Spirits they believed to be lost and forbidden to enter the Spirit World. What more could they do? They were subservient women. They had been dependent upon their Braves for the very meat that nourished their bodies. Their Braves were lost. They must place their faith intensely upon the inclination of the Great Spirit.

Their faith did not waver as their children whimpered and died painfully of starvation. The women reasoned that life's suffering had come to an end for their beloved children. It was so as their children had been introduced to the Great Spirit at birth by the tribal Medicine Man.

He no longer lived to guide the children's wandering spirits to the Spirit World with his magic smoke and spells. Therefore, the children's spirits must be conveyed to the Spirit World by their ancestors.

Their faith remained as their bellies grew taut with hunger. Their dreams were pervaded by the sights and smells of meat. They grew lean and frail. Through all these privations, they continued to keep faith; the women believed as one that they must wait for the Great Spirit to manifest his will. This was their only hope for salvation.

Chapter Thirty-Four

The Ancient One lay prostate on the packed dirt floor of her lodge and prayed. Her hair was white, thick, and voluptuous. It reached beneath her waist. She dressed in thick, heavy animal furs. Her blood was icy cold and moved sluggishly through her veins. She shivered and was reminded of a freezing winter morning; it was now high summer.

Her age had not been counted in many turnings of the sun. She had begged the Great Spirit to release her from the pains of living, but he did not answer her prayers. She wondered why this was so. She had been a good woman throughout her long years. How could she continue to live with this terrible pain locked within her useless, aging, and sagging body?

She was known to the Apache Tribe as the Ancient One. The old ones who had the knowledge of her birth name and where she had come from had departed for the Spirit World long ago. The Medicine Man was the last to pass into the Spirit World. He left knowing all her truths, yet he had not revealed this knowledge. The Ancient One was not aware that he had been gifted with a foretelling of her celebrated destiny. He did not inform her. He reasoned that the Great Spirit would reveal this glorious destiny in his own time. He saw that the Apache would survive only if they believed Apache blood ran through her veins. It was necessary for her to fulfill her destiny. He had been wise.

As the Ancient One prayed, her memories carried her into her past. She had been stolen in an Apache raid against her village. She was large with child and a beautiful young woman. She could remember it clearly. Her features were finely made; they were not round and flat like her people's features. Her hair was shining black and very long; it reached to her knees. Her eyes were luminous pools of blackness. They sparkled with unshed tears. Yet they were enraged beneath the tears, and they shone like a stack of burning coals. She saw the fires and smelled the smoke as her people's huts burned. She heard their screams and their pleadings to be left with their lives. She could see many members of her family running to escape into the Black Hills. Her facial expression remained brave and stoic as her people would expect of her, but her heart was breaking.

Her people had existed as a peaceful tribe belonging to the Black Hills Nation. They existed quietly with many other tribes. Their livelihood was based on trade of the precious gold they mined in the Black Hills. They exchanged this gold for the necessities of life. They were easily overpowered by the attacking Apaches. The

Apaches had no motivation for the attack, and they took nothing. They came only to destroy.

Once the Apaches satisfied their bloodlust, she was removed to the Apache camp. Even now, she could close her eyes and see the strong brown possessive arms holding her tightly on the overly large speckled horse. There was no escaping this Brave; this Brave claimed her as his own. They galloped, and she could only see blurred unfamiliar scenery through her Black Hills eyes.

This Brave placed her in his hut, and she could not leave. He did not touch her while she carried another's child. She learned it was the Apache way. This she did not expect, but she was grateful. Her lost Black Hills Brave was still within her heart.

She remembered, in time, she came to love this Apache Brave. He was a kind and affectionate man. He passed to the Spirit World during one of the Apaches' endless battles with the white man. She would have no other Brave after his passing. She isolated herself in her hut and grew old.

Her mind took her backward to the birth of her babe. She remembered praying silently and constantly to the Great Spirit. Her heartfelt prayer as she labored was endless.

She spoke, "Please, oh Great One, permit the Apaches to allow my babe to live."

Her son came before the proper time. His cries were loud and healthy. The Apaches refused her simple request to keep him and be his mother. She felt her mother's heart break. She craved to hold him in her arms and give him her breast. She could not understand what harm this could bring. However, it was decided by the Great Chief that this helpless babe should be given back to the Black Hills Nation. He was of Black Hills blood; therefore, he was weak. Apache blood was known for its strength. Once he reached manhood, he would create babes that would result in a weakening of the Apache bloodline.

She had no knowledge of the Apaches' reasoning. She could only remember her relief and joyful thoughts. *The Apache do not kill innocent babes.*

She was at long last given the babe to hold by a compassionate old woman. She kissed him and gave him the name of Shining Star. She whispered in his ear, "I will love you always, my son. I wish you to grow to be a good and faithful man." She was calm as she handed the babe over to the closest Brave. The Apaches thought it odd, but they could not see what her senses had made known to her.

Shining Star was a Black Hills Conjurer and precious to the Great Spirit. His life was guarded. This was the real reason the Apaches did not kill him. She had no doubt that he would be delivered safely. She was sure that he would be protected all his life. She was at peace. She would hear of his life. She was gratified with this much.

Shining Star grew to manhood and took a wife. She was an Apache woman who fled the white man for the killing of her white husband. She was exiled by the Apache who did not wish to bring the white man's wrath upon them. She left the Apache camp with her mother, carrying a babe in a sling made of coyote furs around her neck. Her mother, Bright Star, offered up her life in an act of love to the white man's posse who pursued them. Her self-sacrificing act saved Coyote Hunter and her granddaughter, Prairie Blossom, from certain death.

Coyote Hunter traveled north toward freedom; heavy grief weighed down her heart at the loss of her mother. She was soon captured by a party of Black Hills Braves. Her courage and bravery were displayed and compelled the Medicine Man to adopt her into the Black Hills Nation. He renamed her She Who Dares.

A son was born to Shining Star, a son who was half Apache and half Black Hills, a son approved by the Great Spirit. His name was Geronimo and was bestowed upon him by the Great Spirit. His destiny was written of in the great prophecies. Geronimo would become the greatest chief the Apache Nation would ever know, and he would be the last Conjurer to be born upon the earth.

She did not brag or flaunt that she was grandmother to Geronimo. Her safety lay within the realms of the unnoticed Ancient One. And her wisdom allowed her to see the innate cruelty in Geronimo's nature. She could see that his cruelty was necessary. He must hold Apache land from the greedy and grasping white man. Geronimo and his Braves kept the land safe until they died in mass suicide evading the Great White Chief's ambush. She prayed for forgiveness of their spirits and begged the Great Spirit to allow their entry into the Spirit World.

The Ancient One put her memories aside. She had drifted away to her past while the Apache women were in desperate need. She thought once again, *I am too old, and my remorse is great.* She wept, her tears falling onto the packed dirt floor. She prayed aloud, "Oh Great Spirit, these women are innocent. I beg you to save them from starvation. I do not matter. I am old and of no use. I know you love your creatures. Please do not let these women die before their appointed time."

She felt her head lift of its own accord. Her eyes were wide open in shock. They were locked on her ancient spear in the corner of the lodge. She understood and was stricken with overwhelming terror. She prayed for understanding. "Oh please, Great Spirit, my body is old."

Suddenly, her arthritic joints began to crack and twist as they straightened into the shape of the youthfulness of her past. She made no sound though she was in agony. As the pain subsided, she saw the body of a young woman. Youthful vitality belonging to moons long gone suddenly entered her blood. The coldness of her blood was replaced with glorious heat. With it, a fiery blaze of power raced to her inner spirit.

She was young again.

She stripped her furs off rapidly and replaced them with an old soft leather tunic not worn in many years. She saw that the white hair was left to her to symbolize her wisdom.

She thought, *My wisdom must be apparent to the women if I am to teach them to survive without their*

Braves. I will succeed. I will fulfill the destiny the Great Spirit chose for me.

The Ancient One now believed that this was the reason she had lived so long. She prayed to the Great Spirit with gratitude for the gift of this destiny and the gift of youth. Her newfound usefulness brought her much pleasure. She prayed with deep repentance for all the times she had begged to die.

She sprinted easily as she carried her ancient spear to the designated speaking circle. It was compulsory; the women must listen to her while she spoke as she stood in the circle. She stepped into the circle with the agility of a much younger woman. The starving women surrounded her, curiosity in their eyes. The Ancient One was pleased. These women still had mental strength in spite of the dullness that was brought by lack of food.

She sympathized. *It is important I speak with kindness. They have endured much.* Her voice became loud as they must hear her for their survival. She said, "You must hunt. You must fill your bellies with meat."

The women looked longingly at her spear, hope glistening in their dark eyes.

The Ancient One said, "No, I will not hunt for you. I am no Brave. I will teach you to hunt. The Great Spirit has given me agility and strength. He has refreshed my knowledge on your behalf. It is he that has brought me new life."

Bold Feather stepped into the speaking circle. She was a rebellious young woman, but very attractive with her long black hair and sensuous lips. The Ancient One could see that Bold Feather did not hear the voice of the Great Spirit in her dreams. Her character became even more apparent as she responded maliciously to the Ancient One.

She said, "Have you forgotten, Ancient One? We are forbidden to touch weapons except in war!" She implied there was senility in the Ancient One's words. She also implied that the Ancient One did not obey the Great Spirit's wishes.

The Ancient One thrust her spear, point first, deeply into the earth of the speaking circle. She responded in fury laced with stern exasperation, "Who is here to stop us, Bold Feather? You may starve if you wish. These women must choose their own way."

The wisdom within the Ancient One allowed her to see a deeply buried resentment in Bold Feather's dark eyes; she saw the flickering of a small red flame. The Ancient One knew that her trial had begun. She did not expect it to surface so quickly.

The Ancient One prayed silently and quickly for the understanding and the patience she needed. She was rewarded with a foreseeing from the Great Spirit. "You must not fear. Bold Feather will learn to hunt. She will not die of starvation."

The Ancient One saw that she spoke out against the use of spears to oppose what she perceived as the Ancient One's usurped authority over the women. The foreseeing also revealed to the Ancient One that she would meet her death brutally by Bold Feather's hand.

The Ancient One thought, *I must ward against my impending death, I must teach the women to hunt, I must cultivate my courage, and I must accept death's com-*

ing at its appointed time. Death must be met with love, forgiveness, and above all, courage. I will reach the Spirit World. I will.

The Ancient One reasserted herself quickly. She must put to use her store of wisdom; she must examine closely what pertinent things she had learned in her long life.

She knew there were two inescapable laws derived from the cycle of birth to death. She thought, *The first law is a natural truth. The young are driven to challenge the old. The second law is the greatest truth of all, bringing with it a soothing benevolence against Bold Feather's resentment. All that live must die.*

The Ancient One waited in the speaking circle during these contemplations. Her spear remained buried. She would not attempt to persuade the women. Even so, she saw the women's eyes sparkle with hope, expectation, and initiative. They perceived the opportunity offered by the Ancient One through the wishes of the Great Spirit. They could learn to hunt large game with much fat and meat. They would feed themselves.

Without prompting, the women began a search in the camp for the spears left behind by their Braves. Their search was fruitful. There were many spears made for different uses. The women were now well-equipped and very impatient to learn.

The Ancient One spoke, "We will begin at sunrise. I promise you, if the Great Spirit wills, we will eat meat at moonrise."

She turned to leave the speaking circle. All could hear a loud rumbling in the distance. This was the buffalo migrating to the Apache hunting grounds. There was a loud whooping from the women.

They called out, "We will follow you, Ancient One. The Great Spirit is with you. He has brought the buffalo to prove the truth of your words."

Chapter Thirty-Five

Once the Ancient One returned to her hut, there was whispering among the women to one another. Bold Feather had demanded to be given the heaviest and longest buffalo spear. The women were not surprised. Bold Feather had always pushed herself forward in an attempt to make others feel small in the hope of impressing the Apache Braves.

But Bold Feather had never belonged to a Brave. The Braves had seen her character plainly. They had declined her flirtatious offers with amusement. "We want no woman who will wear a man's headdress." This memory caused the women to chuckle quietly. This comment meant that their value was appreciated. However, their grief returned to them shortly as they remembered their great loss.

The Ancient One returned to her hut to meditate on the destiny given by the Great Spirit. It would be a difficult but rewarding destiny. She threw her youthful body onto the floor and prayed. "Thank you, Great Spirit, for trusting me with this destiny. I will not disappoint you. I have been gifted with youth and wisdom. It is a miraculous wonder to feel my blood rushing through my veins. Wisdom, I have acquired through ancientness. My youth fled from me long ago, Great Spirit. This gift you have given to me freely. My purpose in life has always been to obey your will. You have given me the chance to enter the Spirit World as one who was chosen. My heart is full of thankfulness, oh Great One."

She must think about the women. Tomorrow, they will hunt buffalo. The Ancient One wished for more than one buffalo. Once dried, it would keep many moons. But how to teach them to hunt the buffalo?

The words echoed in her mind: "One footstep and then another."

She whispered, "Thank you, Great Spirit."

The Ancient One understood that buffalos were not easy to kill. Her only option was to teach the women to use the old ways of hunting with a spear. The women must coat their bodies with the precious buffalo fat that had kept them alive for so long. A buffalo's eyesight is weak, but their noses are keen. This would bring the scent of buffalo, and there would be no alarm among the herd.

The women must use all their wiles. They must work together in groups. They must creep, backs bent, and wearing a buffalo hide; they must not rise higher from the ground than the buffalo, or they would be recognized as a threat by the buffalo. Their spears must remain close to their bodies, hidden and pointing toward the ground.

Without mounts, protection for the women would not be provided by the horse's body, nor was there height leverage for thrusting their spears. They must use all of their body's strength. Using a spear and stabbing in an inexact place only enrages a buffalo; they will become dangerous and attack. The women must seek a quick kill by puncturing the spinal cord at the base of the buffalo's neck.

A group of women must be located in front and to each side of the weakly ones. These buffalo cannot keep up with the herd or run as fast. Another group of women must be located behind the weakly buffalo. The women in front must be on guard that they do not cause the buffalo to run in the wrong direction and trample the women behind.

The Ancient One was sure these buffalo had been hunted by many different tribes, including the white man. They would recognize a spear or rifle lifted high for killing. The women must not choose strong buffalo, and above all, not an old cow. She is full of wile and protective of her herd; she is fast and deadly.

The Ancient One meditated and prayed most of the night. She then scouted the buffalo herd. She saw that the Great Spirit had provided a ravine climbable for the women, but deadly for the buffalo. She was joyful. Their first hunt would be much easier than she had anticipated. The Ancient One thought, *Thanks be to the Great Spirit*.

It was time to wake the women. After the hunt, she would have them practice driving the spear into the spinal cord once the buffalo had been driven off the ravine. She would teach them the art of killing on the lame buffalo lying at the base of the ravine. These women were intelligent, courageous, intuitive, and confident. There was much to teach, but her pupils were motivated by great need. She did not believe it would be difficult for her or for them. The Ancient One felt it was the will of the Great Spirit that these women succeed. She was confident that by moon's rising, the women would eat their fill of red, fatty, succulent meat, and the sheen of buffalo fat would coat their faces.

The Ancient One was grateful, but in her great store of wisdom, she also carried a profound sadness within her heart. Her destiny was comprised of many facets. She saw plainly through the eyes of many other living tribes. This was a serious act she was committing. She was creating a new cultural tribe of Apache women. She could easily visualize these women when they acquired the skills necessary to survive. She saw clearly that knowledge gives power to the beholder. This knowledge would remain with them always. It would be their choice in what manner they used this knowledge.

The Ancient One thought, *The Great Spirit allows us all free will. Some of these women would yearn for love and would find it again. These would be the fortunate ones.*

But as life would have it, many would lose much more. These ones would never be subservient women again. A Brave's hearth would be lost to them throughout the rest of their lives. They would drift away.

"It is out of my hands," the Ancient One concluded. This could not be corrected by any other than the Great Spirit. She decided not to worry about these women and their possible futures. They would survive, regardless of the path they chose to follow. She would trust in the Great Spirit and fulfill her destiny.

Chapter Thirty-Six

The moon faded as the Texas sky began to lighten. The sun peeked over the horizon. The Ancient One thought, *The time has come to awaken the women*.

They arose with vigor and rubbed the sleep from their eyes. Their awakening was filled with eagerness and excitement; they chattered and daydreamed of much meat to fill their bellies. The Ancient One had promised meat by moonrise, and all knew the Great Spirit was with her. They questioned each with assurance, "Didn't he bring the buffalo once she had spoken?"

The Ancient One strode to the speaking circle. It was her signal for silence. It was time to begin the teaching and the learning.

Bold Feather turned her back and walked quickly away. The Ancient One could see that she did not move beyond hearing distance. The women quieted their gleeful prattling. They faced the Ancient One with expressions of determination blended with a desperate need to gain the independence they must have to survive.

The Ancient One examined them closely. She felt great pride in her pupils. She thought, *These women are courageous. They will go forth to hunt buffalo. They are wise in many ways.* The Ancient One did not need to explain that hunting buffalo was dangerous and difficult; many of their Braves had died in the attempt. The Ancient One could feel their fear. She also could see that their craving for this knowledge overpowered their fear. Their resolve eased her spirit. She was sure they would learn to hunt the buffalo brought by the Great Spirit.

The Ancient One thought carefully about her contemplation of the women. She concluded that it was the right time to begin teaching. She spoke in a loud, powerful voice, "Women, coat your bodies and the hides of your sleeping furs with buffalo fat."

The women obeyed immediately. They knew of this; they observed the Braves using the fat of the buffalo to camouflage their scent. Their faith in the Ancient One's wisdom doubled.

Bold Feather reached into the leather pouch with stealth and retrieved a large handful.

The Ancient One thought, *She is following my direction, but does not wish for me or the others to observe her.* She then continued, "You have completed this task, but I must teach you more. Women, tie your hunting spears inside of your hides with rawhide strips."

The women looked bewildered but spoke no words and accomplished this task quickly and efficiently. This step was a temporary precaution, but necessary for novices. The women must cover their bodies at all times with the hides as they stalked the buffalo. It is imperative that they do not drop their hide coverings or their spear. This step assured their hands remained free to cover themselves with their hide. Through many hunts, they would naturally learn to hold their spears securely.

The Ancient One spoke, "I must speak, and you must listen, not only with your ears, but with your heart as well. We will creep up on the sickly and weakly located at the rear of the grazing buffalo herd. We will remove our spears for our own protection. You will surround them and separate them from the herd. We will spook the buffalo by swinging our capes and whooping loudly. The healthy herd will stampede, and the weakly buffalo will attempt to follow. You must not allow the weakly ones to follow. The Great Spirit has provided a ravine for us. We must drive these weakly ones into the ravine." She explained to the starving women, "It is necessary that we must work together and quickly. These weakly ones must not be allowed to escape. If this should happen, you will not eat meat this moonrise. Show your bravery and do all I have said. Let us hunt."

The women quietly moved to the hunting grounds with the Ancient One in the lead. All were garbed in their hides. They crept to the back of the herd. There they saw the weakly ones and the ravine.

THE CHOSEN ONES

The Ancient One spoke quietly, "We shall pray. Dear Great Spirit, please allow us to capture these buffalo, and please keep us protected against injury if it is your will." She then ordered in a bare whisper, "Women, remove your spears and keep them pointed at the ground."

It was rapidly accomplished.

She then ordered, "Surround the buffalo and swing your hides and whoop loudly. You must not lose sight of the ravine."

The women surrounded the buffalo. As if they were of one mind, they began to swing their capes and frighten the buffalos with their whooping. The main herd stampeded as the Ancient One had said they would. The women in front drove the sickly buffalo back, and the women in the back merged with the women on each side, driving the buffalo toward the ravine. The women near the mouth of the ravine split and opened a path to trick the buffalo. The buffalo saw a safe escape in this route and stampeded toward this open path. At the mouth of the ravine, they halted suddenly, sensing danger.

Bold Feather suddenly appeared between the herd and the ravine. The Ancient One was not surprised. She taunted them with her swinging hide, her whooping, and impromptu dancing. The buffalo became angry and lost their sense of danger. They interpreted her actions as a challenge. They stamped and scratched their hooves as a warning to her; clouds of dusty Texas grime permeated the air. Bold Feather began to back away toward the mouth of the ravine. She used body language to speak of her terror. She did not feel terror; all could see she was glowing with battle rage. The buffalo charged her as if their minds were one. Bold Feather leapt to safety at the last instant. The Ancient One admitted that she barely missed being trampled by the buffalo. She allowed that Bold Feather was not lacking courage. She simply said, "Blood will tell."

The rest of the women leaped forward and kept the herd moving by whooping and swinging their capes. The buffalo were driven into and over the ravine by a new tribe of hide-slinging whooping women.

The women were proud and ecstatic as they gazed down into the ravine. There were many buffalo piled on top of each other. Most were dead, but many were lame and attempting to rise.

The women, with no prompting from the Ancient One, climbed down into the ravine and began to kill the wounded. The Great Spirit did not want his creatures to suffer, and these women heard his voice. They killed swiftly and with compassion. This task was completed soon. They returned to the Ancient One for further instructions.

The Ancient One spoke proudly, "Fearless women, you have done well. The Great Spirit is with you. We must pray and give our thanks to the Great Spirit and the buffalos' spirit for providing us with this nourishment." She prayed, "Oh Great One, we give you much gratitude and great appreciation. You have saved these weakling women from starvation for many moons. Please allow the spirits belonging to the buffalo to see only gratitude in our hearts."

The Ancient One called out, "Victorious women, retrieve the sled and begin butchering. Haul everything back to the communal lodge. Begin the preserving process. Do not waste anything. All of you have done these chores for generations. You will not need me. My body is tired. I must rest in my hut. Well done, Bold Feather. You saved the hunt."

Bold Feather flushed overly with pride and lacking modesty.

She will always be arrogant, yet she has much courage, thought the Ancient One.

The Ancient One departed. The women chattered as they worked. The hunt was done, and the women would eat meat as the Ancient One had promised. Their gratitude was immense, not only for the meat, but to the Great Spirit and his bringing of the Ancient One to save them.

The women butchered until sunset while Bold Feather retrieved the sled. It would be seasoned, dried, and preserved in many ways unique only to the Apache. The women would eat well for many moons. The women's sparkling eyes reflected their happiness. There would be a great feast at moonrise.

The Ancient One collapsed on her sleeping roll. She felt her youthful vigor depleting from her body. She saw that she had fulfilled her destiny. Her time had finally come. She was so cold.

She reflected on the hunt. She saw that Bold Feather was the next destined chosen one. *She must mature. It will be my task to guide her. She has courage but lacks the respect of the women. They feel no cause to respect her, even for her spontaneous movements that saved the hunt. Her measures saved them from starvation. They saw her behavior as another Bold Feather effort designed to make them feel small.*

It was so, but the Ancient One saw that she behaved with great courage also. The women did not reach out a hand to help her.

Bold Feather will need what wisdom I can provide. It will be a tedious chore. All know the young are blind. She chastised herself firmly, "You must have faith in the Great Spirit."

It was true that Bold Feather would change little and would always need to battle the arrogant nature in her blood. The Ancient One must restrain her. Bold Feather must receive the respect of the women if she wishes to complete her destiny successfully. All must respect their teacher to learn. And the women must learn to survive.

The Ancient One's sufferings led her to wish for Bold Feather and her strength of will. She wanted to end this terrible pain of aging at such a rapid pace. She could feel her joints swelling and twisting and the cold and sluggishness of her blood as it moved through her veins and arteries. Her only hope was Bold Feather. She called to Bold Feather with her mind, knowing she would hear her. The Ancient One had known long ago that Bold Feather was her great-granddaughter, bearing the mental powers common to their bloodline. Bold Feather would come to end her suffering. *She will understand my need to pass quickly and with dignity.*

THE CHOSEN ONES

Bold Feather rapped on the hut's door almost instantly. She was panting from lack of breath. She ran the lengthy path to the Ancient One's hut.

The Ancient One said in weakness, "Please help me, Bold Feather."

Bold Feather entered the hut. Her face was still as she saw the aging on the Ancient One's body and face. Bold Feather could see she was dying slowly and painfully. She knew this form of lingering death was dreaded by all Apache. Bold Feather said, "I will help you, Ancient One."

Bold Feather had learned a small part of her past and possible future from her mother, Pearl, who had died when Bold Feather was a grown child, but still very far from adulthood. At Pearl's diseased deathbed, she told Bold Feather she was Geronimo's daughter. Geronimo did not have this knowledge of having a daughter. Pearl had not told him, and he did not suspect. Pearl did not want Bold Feather to be used as a pawn in the white man's ruses.

Bold Feather became arrogant and superior to other females upon receiving this knowledge. She believed it would make no difference. She did not know as a child that it would make all of the difference.

She bent down and kissed her great-grandmother on the lips. She said, "I have known long that you are my great-grandmother. You have left me alone all of my life, and I have learned to love you in spite of your self-imposed isolation. You have called on me to end your suffering as I did with the buffalo. I will do this thing."

Bold Feather removed her butchering knife and rapidly slit her great-grandmother's throat. She led her into the Spirit World by speaking words of a distant love to encourage her to let go of her body.

When the Ancient One's spirit left her body, there was a golden blaze of color for a bare instant. Bold Feather felt a sense of rightness. She was absolved of killing kin by the Great Spirit; he allowed her to see the Ancient One's spirit fly to the Spirit World. She had received the Ancient One's memories, qualities, and wisdom upon her death. Yes, it was a sign for Bold Feather. Now, she must look out for the women and eventually lead them to independence. She would carry on the Ancient One's destiny. It had become her destiny.

Bold Feather burnt the hut to the ground. This would ensure there would be no questions to answer and would preserve the Ancient One's dignity.

Bold Feather thought, *I will lead the women to independence. It is my right as Geronimo's daughter.*

The Ancient One spoke in Bold Feather's mind, "It cannot be done until the women accept you. You must earn their respect."

Bold Feather spoke, "I will do this. I will show them I have changed into the Ancient One. I will be patient with the women. I have learned much from you. Your wisdom will guide me."

The Ancient One did not speak, but she was sure Bold Feather did not understand how true this will prove to be.

Chapter Thirty-Seven

Bold Feather transformed her arrogant ways. She brought into being her new personality. She was pleasant and kind to the women. She was intelligent yet patient with those less intelligent. She was calm, thoughtful, moderate, and most of all, she was courageous.

The women respected Bold Feather's individuality. The women believed that Bold Feather could now hear the Great Spirit, but in reality, she heard the Ancient One. They insisted to one another, as women will do, that Bold Feather had changed. They saw that her heart had turned from black spitefulness to a golden warmth.

They whispered to one another, "The Ancient One has come to life again in Bold Feather."

The Ancient One was of the Spirit World and wished to remain there. Even now, she craved to return to that wonderful place. But she must teach Bold

Feather if the women were to become independent and survive.

Bold Feather learned the art of bow and arrow making from the Ancient One. She shared this knowledge with the women. She did not need to explain the uses of the bow and arrow, only their making. This knowledge had belonged only to their Braves.

Bold Feather encouraged the women, through the Ancient One, to choose an arrow fletching that brought power to them. Many women chose to use the same fletching as their lost Braves.

Bold Feather climbed the branches of a scruffy old pine to reach the golden feathers lining the large hawk's nest abandoned at the end of the spring moon. She spoke a silent prayer of thankfulness to the mother hawk for the bounty she received. These feathers would bring her much power. She intended that these golden feathers break her free of the Ancient One's influence, and she would gain more control over the women. Sadly, Bold Feather did not see she was fighting the will of the Great Spirit. Her arrogance made her blind. This was the beginning of the evilness in Bold Feather.

The Ancient One felt a deep sadness at this attempt. She wept. "What is the will of the Great Spirit for this act of defiance? I must not ask. He will accomplish his will in his own time."

Bold Feather's words, spoken through the Ancient One, earned her much respect from her sisters. They were sure in their hearts that the Ancient One lived in Bold Feather. They began to listen and to see that she had gained much wisdom for one so young. She was only twenty-two turnings of the sun, but her spoken words showed a maturity far beyond her years.

They grasped that she still had much to teach them. These women were sure their security lay in her spoken words.

Bold Feather's sisters came to her for more and more knowledge. When this occurred, the Ancient One called to Bold Feather and reminded her that she must make the women independent. It was her true destiny. She must not make them dependent upon her. These women must go when they were ready.

Bold Feather developed a possessive love for her sisters in spite of the powers of the Ancient One. She could not see that this love was based on her selfish nature. She felt a self-importance when her sisters came to her. She was only mindful of this. She wanted not only to rule her sisters, but to be the one to care for their needs. She wished to make life simpler and gentler for these women and to receive much credit.

She desired to provide them with a variety of vegetables and different meats to supplement their diet of buffalo meat. In order for Bold Feather's desire to come about, they would need mounts to reach the far-off woodlands to harvest the wild growing vegetables. They would hunt the animals that were common to these regions.

Bold Feather asked of herself with genuine puzzlement, "How can this come to pass?"

She heard the voice of the Ancient One in her mind. "You must trade."

Bold Feather was shocked. Such a simple solution had been hidden in the depths of her mind for many moons. She questioned herself in confusion, "Why did this solution hide from me? There could be no real reason. Don't I know my mind and my motives? This is very confusing to me."

She could not see her selfishness and arrogance was uppermost in her desire to keep the women dependent. Bold Feather had not wished to see this solution. There would be a large possibility that the women would leave. Mounts would bring independence to the women. They had learned all that could be taught.

The Ancient One saw Bold Feather's heart and mind. She saw Bold Feather's mind pass over what would happen and that she would focus on her own feelings of importance to the women. She would have been wiser in her motives to have examined this solution much closer. The Ancient One smiled knowingly.

Bold Feather's mind skipped ahead to trade details. She began making plans. They would trade with the Black Hills tribe. There were countless buffalo hides and much meat in the drying shed. Yes, they could trade for mounts. Until then, the women must walk to the Black Hills Tribe, pulling many sleds. Another idea occurred to Bold Feather; she must go to the speaking circle and talk to the women. Her excitement was great; she would impress these women with her wonderful ideas.

Bold Feather raced into the speaking circle. Her sisters rapidly surrounded the circle. Bold Feather called out, "Dear sisters of mine, we must trade. We must make our lives better. Please listen and see the wisdom in my words. We have much buffalo meat and many hides. If we owned horses, we could travel to the woodlands for wild growing foods and hunt what becomes meat for us.

"Included with the buffalo meat, we must use our secrets of Apache craft making. All know Apaches are skilled at creating beautiful things. We must create sleeping rolls, tunics, and moccasins out of the excess hides. We must make cooking and eating utensils out of the clay pit near the riverbank. The Apache skills of painting are desirable to the eye. The abundance of quartz made it possible to decorate these objects into an undeniable state of beauty. Our articles must be stunning. One article must be traded for one horse. We must not alter this condition if we all wish to be mounted."

Bold Feather continued, "We must trade with the Black Hills Tribe. Trade is their livelihood. They are sharp traders and will take all for nothing. We, as women, must outwit them. We are Apache. We will obtain our mounts."

A bold young woman stepped into the speaking circle. She was known as Deep Waters. Her long fine black hair swayed in the breeze. She was sixteen summers old, yet her body was a woman's. Her black eyes were slightly slanted and hooded. Deep Waters' thoughts did not flash from her eyes, but she was intelligent. She was quiet, yet she was energetic in her movements. She was tall for an Apache woman and still growing as fast as the Texas prickly pear cacti. In many ways, she was an enigma to the Apache.

She spoke with the soft sweetness of youth. "I do not need to mull this over in my mind. I say we must trade."

The others began to shout, "Yes! Yes!"

Deep Waters spoke no more; she hurried to the communal lodge. If one did not know her nature, they would believe she was embarrassed for stepping forward with her words. But there was much more to Deep Waters than the eye beheld. She simply wished to begin her creations.

The women followed behind her, walking rapidly as if they could not wait to get started.

Bold Feather could see that every creation would be lovely. The Black Hills Tribe would want them. She was certain. She said to herself happily, "We will have mounts soon. We may travel long distances, look for new prospects, and have a variety of food."

As the sunrises passed, Bold Feather began to give more thought to trading. She finally saw the possibilities of the women leaving her. She began to fear. In her mind, she saw it was good to trade, but she began to doubt if it was right for the women.

The Ancient One knew that she doubted if it was right for her, but she did not open her mind. Bold Feather's worry was with her simply because she did not allow herself to see that she was overprotective, assuming, arrogant, and fearful.

Bold Feather began to notice that Apache women were very beautiful. Their beauty would lead to many of the women to stay with the Black Hills Tribe if they were approached by a lusting Brave. These women will want to find love and have children again.

Bold Feather was saddened deep in her heart. Her destiny would not allow her to have a life with a Brave and to have children. She wanted that life, she had always wanted it, but she had let her arrogance leave her in a state of loneliness.

She began to justify these feelings of possessiveness. Surely, she must not leave her sisters to fend for themselves? She would not reach the Spirit World if she were to do this terrible thing. She must explain this to any Black Hills Brave who approached her. They would understand. It was she who led the women.

The Ancient One spoke loudly in Bold Feather's mind, "Bold Feather, this is the ending of your destiny. It is hard to let go. I can help you if you wish to see and hear. You must guard your heart from the arrogance that flows through your blood. Your concern is for yourself, not for your sisters."

Bold Feather could not reason; all her fears sprang from a great fear of abandonment. This blocked her thoughts. She had forgotten that the Great Spirit allowed free will to all his creatures.

The Ancient One spoke to Bold Feather's mind, "Oh, great-granddaughter of mine, you will meet your end if you do not shake off this terrible fear and open up your mind. Can you not see that you will go your own way just as these women will?" The Ancient One kept her thoughts shuttered after this outburst. She saw that Bold Feather could not hear her words.

Bold Feather refused to see that her sisters were independent women. They would leave Bold Feather very soon; they had learned to do all that she taught them. Once the women were mounted, they would go their own way. They would be well-protected with the knowledge given to them. The women saw this knowledge would enable them to survive. They were grateful to be taught this knowledge. But some would look for a home and love; others would love the freedom that came with aloneness. They would live their lives as they wished. It was the Apache way. Bold Feather must accept this truth or die.

The Ancient One wept. "I cannot help Bold Feather make her choices. She will be evil and bring evil upon herself. These things will occur. Bold Feather will not complete her destiny, I will depart from her mind out of necessity, and Bold Feather will not have her heart's desire. All of this is the will of the Great Spirit."

Chapter Thirty-Eight

Bold Feather's fear was laced with astonishment as she watched the women work. They created beauty at an unwavering speed. Bold Feather could see that this camp was not restful to them with the loss of their Braves. She thought, *They have not spoken these words to me, but their actions do speak to me. I have done all for them, can they not see this?* They did see, but their lives were their own.

The handicrafts were stacking up in an organized manner in the communal lodge. Sleeping rolls, one on top of each other in the left side of the room, moccasins below, bows and arrows on the right, clay vessels and utensils below them. The women's thoughtfulness consisted of the addition of clay containers packed with dried prairie grass to store the clay vessels and utensils. These would protect them from breakage and make them stackable for traveling. These containers were decorated beautifully, and this made them usable for many items stored in a Black Hills lodge. Bold Feather could see that these containers would be wanted badly.

The name of the designer was written on the articles, but placed in an area not easily seen. The women were modest. Bold Feather thought this was remarkable; their talent was immense, yet their pride was displayed discreetly on their beautiful creations. This she could not understand.

The women continued to work constantly. Again, Bold Feather felt confusion. *Why is this camp such a beehive? They need not hurry so. I should tell them they must not become worn. Why do they wish to leave me?* However, Bold Feather did see in a remote place in her heart that they wished to leave all they had known before. Terrible memories and feelings would be left in this camp. These items created by them will give them a better life and bring them happiness. These thoughts brought Bold Feather's overwhelming fear back threefold. She could not see that they must leave her and live their lives as they chose.

These thoughts brought a kernel of stubbornness, a misguided sense of rightness, and a manipulative evil took root in Bold Feather's heart. She became determined to do all she could to bring the women back to her.

The Ancient One sensed the change in Bold Feather's heart. She thought, *Bold Feather will use any method to accomplish this terrible desire she has allowed to grow into fruitfulness. Yes, blood will tell. Bold Feather is much like her father.*

THE CHOSEN ONES

In spite of her wisdom, the Ancient One was distressed by what she saw in Bold Feather. She prayed, "Oh Great One, please allow me to help Bold Feather overcome her fear of abandonment." This prayer brought tears of sorrow to her. She had received a foretelling in return. She thought with great sadness, *Bold Feather will fight for dominancy. She will not let go of these women. They will turn away from her, regardless of Bold Feather's actions to achieve her heart's emotional needs. The women will reach for their own happiness as it should be.* The Ancient One chanted within her mind, *Please, Great Spirit. Please, Great Spirit.*

She was given a foretelling. "There will be one who will create vulnerability in Bold Feather simply by appearing. This one will be evil. Bold Feather will fight out of her own resentment and evilness."

The Ancient One saw further; this evil one belonged to the bloodline of the chosen ones, but was not worthy to be chosen. This one's hatred will not ease; it will grow beyond measure. It will drive her to lead Bold Feather with her on the trail that leads to nothingness.

The Ancient One cleared her mind of grief using the faith that was always with her. She said within herself, "All will happen as it is meant to be. I see this as the will of the Great Spirit and the ending of the chosen bloodline. Bold Feather will fight the conclusion of her destiny. Her fear of abandonment clouds her mind. Bold Feather has lost all knowledge of what it is to be Apache. Apaches do not fear, and they do not show fear. It is the Apache way."

Chapter Thirty-Nine

The women were prepared to begin their journey by sunrise. The sleds were loaded and covered with hides, sheltering and protecting their valuable contents from prying eyes. Each of the women were equipped with bows and arrows. They were determined to reach the Black Hills Nation with their goods intact.

At Bold Feather's urging, each woman grasped a portion of the sled railing and began to pull together. The women were enthusiastic in spite of the pulling and tugging on the heavy sleds. They chattered about the many new sights they would see. They tossed ribald remarks at one another. Many intended to entice a lusty Brave into accommodating their neglected needs.

Bold Feather walked in front, leading the progression. She allowed the knowledge of the correct trails to be given to her from the Ancient One, but she had shut the Ancient One's words from her mind. She saw clearly that the Ancient One did not approve of her plans to bring the women back with her. Bold Feather's fears continued to heat and ferment within her heart.

They became more powerful with each step taken. In response to her fears, she would toss her head pridefully, as if she were confident and without a care. She did not help at pulling the sleds. The women took note of this, each to their own thoughts.

There would be much suffering through many sunrises for them to reach the Black Hills trading camp. Upon learning this, the women's moods were not affected, even though pulling the heavy sleds would cause delays. They prattled about their designs and how these items would be wanted by the Black Hills women for use in their lodges. They daydreamed and sighed with a wistful happiness of the many Black Hills Braves trading only to bring his sweetheart a beautiful gift.

They were full of excitement, yet they spoke in low tones. They had noticed a change in Bold Feather. She was more like the Bold Feather they had known long ago. The women questioned one another, "Has the Ancient One departed from her?"

Others answered indignantly, "The Ancient One would not leave us now. Bold Feather is only thoughtful and a bit impatient. She has done much for us. She has made us independent. We would have died without her and the Ancient One. Give thanks to the Great Spirit for the Ancient One and Bold Feather."

The women who questioned felt shame and begged for forgiveness of their sisters.

Only one remained silent. She thought, *Again, I must go unnoticed*. This one had always been in Bold

Feather's shadow, yet she thought she had as much right to be in the lead as Bold Feather. She too felt pulling a stubborn sled was beneath her. Her resentment was building with every tug.

This one was secretive, angry, and as poisonous as a scorpion. She began to daydream. Her secret would make itself known very soon. She must be patient and only await the day of reckoning.

The Ancient One continued to weep. Her thoughts did not change. *Yes, blood will tell. Geronimo's legacy comprised of two beautiful women whose lives would end. They were arrogant, black hearted, and evil. The Great Spirit has left these women. Neither woman will receive his protection. They will not live long.* The Ancient One was sure her prophecy would be proven true.

GREAT CHIEF SHINING STAR

In order to be wise,
We must first be foolish.
—Unknown

Chapter Forty

The women triumphantly reached the boundaries of the Black Hills Nation. They caught sight of well-armed scouts in the distance.

Bold Feather spoke, "These Braves will not harm us. They will only inform the tribunal that we are on their land. You may expect visitors of authority shortly. Remain quiet. I will speak with them."

The Ancient One overcame Bold Feather's mind. "No, I will speak with my people. You will keep quiet."

The women saw Bold Feather's face become red with rage. They did not see or hear why this rage should exist. They were perplexed and fretting to one another in bare whispers, "Why is Bold Feather so angry? We have done nothing wrong, yet she is the Bold Feather of old. Where is the Ancient One? Surely she would not desert us."

A welcoming party appeared sooner than expected. It was not possible to mistake the Great Chief. Turquoise beads decorated his headband, fawn tunic, and moccasins and formed beautiful designs. He was under full headdress. The dyed black eagle feathers lay beneath his white horse's tethers. His unbound shining silver hair contrasted effectively with the black of his headdress; it escaped behind him to rebound on his horse's rump as he cantered to the surviving women. The Medicine Man and the Magic Man accompanied him at a respectful distance, their dress nearly as ornate as this impressive chief's.

The women were reminded of their lost Braves, and sadness permeated their facial expressions; silent and abundant tears rolled down their faces. Many had hopes of becoming a Brave's woman again, to have children again, and to be held at night again. These memories overpowered the women, though they remained silent; heartfelt feelings glistened in their eyes. Others permitted desolation to be present in their eyes. These ones slumped forward in defeat. They believed this Great Chief would turn them away. They saw that they were only women. Who would want them?

Each woman heard the voice of the Ancient One. "Women, your worth is measured by me. You have choices. The Great Spirit gives us all free will. Your worth as women has doubled. Show pride."

Their bodies straightened as one. They realized their pride was all they owned. That realization was followed by another.

They whispered, "The Ancient One is back. Give thanks to the Great Spirit."

The Great Chief arrived and examined the women with sharp, black, and wise eyes. The old chief had planned to turn them away. It was the ruling of the tribunal. He saw their tears, he saw what they had accomplished as women alone, and he could not bring it into his heart to turn them away. Yet he must maintain good relations with the tribunal. He saw there was a way to let the women trade while pleasing the tribunal.

He spoke, "Who speaks as the lead woman here?"

Bold Feather spoke in the Ancient One's soft husky voice. "I do, Great Chief."

The Great Chief started. He heard this voice in his dreams. He said, "What is your name, wise one?"

She said, "I am called the Ancient One. My name has been lost throughout the generations, Great Chief. I speak through this young woman's tongue. All know it is best that the young do not speak."

The Great Chief guffawed loudly. He said, "You are indeed wise, Ancient One." He spoke, "I perceive many trade items under those hides. You must not trade in our camp, but you have my permission to move a heap west. My people will come to you. This requirement is because the Apache Braves and their Great Chief Geronimo committed mass suicide. We do not wish to have their lingering spirits in our camp. Will you accept these conditions, Ancient One?"

The Ancient One said, "Yes, gladly, Great Chief. We traveled a great distance on foot. These women wish to trade for mounts, Great Chief."

The Great Chief said, "We have many mounts that we must only feed. My people will be more than willing to meet your wishes, Ancient One."

The Ancient One continued, "Great Chief, we have a gift for you."

A young woman called Nimo brought forth a container decorated beautifully and filled with utensils. The Great Chief inspected this gift and saw it was a gift fit for a chief; he had been honored greatly by these women.

The Magic Man spoke, "I sense much evil, Great Chief."

The Great Chief looked to the Ancient One.

She said, "Yes, Great Chief. There is evil here, but it is of no danger to the Black Hills Nation. It comes from two young women with hate in their hearts. I have had a foretelling. They will destroy one another. Please do not turn us away because of two misguided women who do not hear the Great Spirit."

The Medicine Man spoke, "Both of these women are the spawn of Geronimo, Great Chief. They will destroy each other as Geronimo destroyed himself. There will be great pain for the Ancient One to endure."

The Magic Man spoke, "The Ancient One speaks truth, Great Chief. This evil has nothing to do with us. It is for her to endure. They are her great-granddaughters."

The Ancient One spoke, "When their deaths occur, it will be the ending of my destiny. I must only complete the Great Spirit's will as his last faithful chosen one adopted into Apache Nation. The rest of the women can and will do as they wish with their lives. I am thankful that I may return to the Spirit World soon."

The Great Chief spoke, "I thank you, Ancient One, for this beautiful gift and for the gift of the truth. We will depart. Expect my people soon." He wheeled his horse around and galloped away to the Black Hills camp. The Ancient One's voice nagged within his mind. He thought, *Who is she? I feel as if she has been with me always. If it is the Great Spirit's will, I will learn this truth.* He was trailed by the Magic Man and the Medicine Man.

The Ancient One directed the women. "Travel west, worn women, for only a short way and set up camp. It will soon be time to trade." The Ancient One thought, *The evil ones must do battle. I may then depart for the Spirit World.* She was sure of this truth. She did not know that the Great Spirit would provide her with a much-loved reward for her faithful service as his chosen one of the Apaches.

Chapter Forty-One

The Great Chief Shining Star gave permission for the Black Hills tribe to begin trading as he revealed his precious gift. Exclamations of beauty were spoken in voices of restrained excitement. The tribal members wished to own such precious items. They asked their Great Chief, "What must we offer to obtain items of this worth?"

Chief Shining Star said, "These women will trade for healthy and strong mounts."

The tribal members scurried to the impromptu trading grounds tugging their surplus mounts behind them.

Chief Shining Star was unsure of his reasons for helping these lost women. His heart told him that he wanted to see them succeed and that they must succeed. He thought, *Is this due to the Ancient One whose voice still haunts me?* This thought brought more questions. It was evident that these women had suffered much.

He saw that these women were not soft and weak as women should be; they were wiry and strong, and they carried weapons.

The Great Chief spoke to his Holy Men, "I have not seen a warrior tribe of women in my long lifetime. Yet that is what many of them appear to be. I am impressed. These women have not only survived, they have excelled. Yet they show a quiet pride in their achievements.

"Many of them are still gentle women, needing the love of a Brave. Some are far different. Regardless, they are no longer the submissive Apache Woman. They are survivors now."

His line of thought changed abruptly.

He said, "Am I helping them because I saw their sad, tear-streaked faces? Or is it because of their accomplishments as abandoned women that has brought me this profound respect?"

Chief Shining Star was not enticed by the giving of the skillful imaginative gift. A gift was only to be expected in return for his kindness in allowing them to trade. He thought, *The gift itself is an example of the resourcefulness of these women. I will go to the steam hut with the Medicine Man and the Magic Man for meditation. I will pray for answers to my questions.*

Chief Shining Star felt his muscles relax and his body cleanse as clouds of steam rolled over the men. He had discussed his thoughts with the Medicine Man and the Magic Man.

Their answers had been informative. "Chief Shining Star, you must allow the Great Spirit to work through you. Your impulse to help these women has been driven through your heart intentionally. The Great Spirit will provide you with answers in good time."

The Great Chief recognized the wisdom of their soft-spoken words. These words made him see that the Great Spirit was guiding his hand. He prayed silently, expressing his gratitude to be judged as a worthy tool. He would be patient. He would have his answers in the proper place and time.

Chapter Forty-Two

The Black Hills Tribe began to arrive. The people approached the spur-of-the-moment trading grounds in dribs and drabs. The women hurriedly arranged the objects on the terrain; they were far enough apart for each item to be easily seen and examined from all sides. All was set up and completed for these traders.

The Ancient One had directed the women in the formation of a circle of truth. This circle was drawn with sharp sticks in the earth surrounding an enormous area. It was composed of many other circles crisscrossing each other. It symbolized a pledge of honesty for all traders. Cheating or lying within this circle brought the Great Spirit's wrath upon the violator.

Speech between the women and the traders was nearly nonexistent. The Black Hills traders pointed at an article, requesting permission to examine it closely. If they chose this article, a horse was offered for inspection. The horses were examined and found to be in excellent condition and of many different bloodlines. Several tribal members brought more than a single horse to trade. These traders took many items back with them on a sled. Trading was completed rapidly. The result was that all the women owned mounts, and all the articles were in the huts of the Black Hills tribe.

Bold Feather was livid. The Ancient One had full control of her body. She could see some women depart when they received their mounts. They sought a better life. She could hear them take leave of the Ancient One with words of gratitude and love. These women did not address or recognize Bold Feather in any way. To them, she was unseen. She thought resentfully, *I have done much for these women, and they leave me without a word.*

The women could perceive the Ancient One's influence brought out the temporary goodness in Bold Feather's heart. They could perceive Bold Feather's heart had blackened with arrogance. They felt she did no more than the Ancient One directed. Therefore, they owed her nothing.

There were women who did not leave. A group of women waited with hopeful shining eyes. They desired to have love and children again. During trading, they had received much interest from many Braves. They would wait for these Braves to approach them. They were sure, as all women are, that it would not be long. At moonrise, the sound of horses galloping came to their ears. Many young Braves arrived and vaulted off their horses.

A Brave came forward and drew a speaking circle on the earth. He stepped inside the circle and spoke.

"I speak for all of the Braves here. Most of us have no women. Our mates have succumbed to the white man's disease. We wish for a mate to share our hut. We can see that Apache women are beautiful, strong, and independent. We wish for willing women to step forward and stand before the Brave you have favored to be your mate."

The bolder women walked quickly forward to stand beside their chosen Brave. Shyer women followed behind them meekly.

Each Brave found that he possessed more than two women. Black Hills tribal law allowed a Brave to have as many mates as he could feed and clothe. These additional mates would live as sisters and maintain peace in the hut. One shall not strive to be favored over another. Punishment for this act was the end of their status as a Brave's mate. These Apache women had shared huts with their sisters for many moons. They craved peace, love, and children.

These fortunate Braves walked side by side with their prospective mates. They walked the trail that led back to the camp. Each Brave held many strong and rough hands. They did not ride away and let their newly won bride walk. This gesture made it known to the women that their newly chosen Braves carried in their hearts an abundance of respect. The silence was comfortable as the women and their Braves walked under a summer moon barely peeking out of a darkening purple sky.

The Medicine Man waited. He would bind them together for as long as they both should wish. It was the Black Hills way.

Chief Shining Star smiled as he lay on his pallet. The sounds of new love and much revelry came to his ears. His memories took him back to the love he shared with She Who Dares and the birthing of their only child, Geronimo.

Shining Star prayed nightly that Geronimo's spirit did not roam the earth. He soon became wretched with desolation at the memories of so much loss. He cried out, "Oh, Great Spirit, please forgive my son Geronimo and the Braves who committed such a vile act. Great Spirit, I have lived too long. I have experienced the death of a favored son and a loving mate. Grief overwhelms me."

After She Who Dares departed to the Spirit World, there had been no other woman for Shining Star. None could take her place, though many women were willing. His heart had moved without restraint at his first sight of her. She was fighting frantically to save her newborn babe. Her courage was remarkable; he loved her so. He wished deep in his soul, "Oh, to be young! To make love to her once more." Tears rolled down his wrinkled old cheeks.

He spoke, "Great Spirit, I do regret that I am much too old for lovemaking and that I have lost my precious mate. I have also lost the lust of a young Brave, but I do remember the closeness and the pleasure of joining with She Who Dares. Oh, Great Spirit, I must stop these melancholy memories and pray for the young ones to find happiness and bring many strong children to the tribe. She Who Dares would wish it so."

He could hear her wise counsel batter his mind. "Yes, my fine husband, you have lost much, but you have gained much in return. Raise your head and be proud."

It was as if she was there with him. He dropped off to sleep, and he had pleasant dreams throughout the night. He woke without melancholy. In his dreams, he shared his sleeping furs with She Who Dares.

Chapter Forty-Three

The moon was now at its peak; torches were alight. The Ancient One still inhabited Bold Feather's body. She thought, *What will happen to the women who chose to stay behind without a Brave?* The Ancient One's thought passed away in a glimmer.

In the twilight and silence, Deep Waters sprang her horse and brought it into a gallop with her fine black hair flying behind her. She halted her mount viciously in the speaking circle. She smiled confidently, secretly, and mysteriously at the remaining women.

She spoke loudly and confidently. "You are left behind as women who do not need or want a Brave. I am one with you. Follow me. We will harry the white man, with good reason. The white man caused this. We have lost much, our fine Apache Braves and our Great Chief, Geronimo."

She saw interest in the eyes of the women and became excited. The Ancient One saw that her new-found freedom arced from her eyes.

She whooped and shouted, "Let us raise havoc among the whites! If you are with me, follow me now." Deep Waters brought her horse into a towering rear and galloped due south. Her followers howled their approval, sprang on their horses, and gouged their horses brutally to pursue Deep Waters.

The Ancient One wept. "Their hearts have not stopped seething. Can they not see they ride to their deaths? The white man is well armed and unyielding. Oh, Great Spirit, I must let this leave my hands and place it in yours. I can only be grateful that my destiny is nearly fulfilled."

Bold Feather was becoming difficult for the Ancient One to contain. She was full of rage and wickedness. Her heart wished to see the women dead rather than find love and happiness. She wished Deep Waters and her followers a lingering death masked as a glorious revenge. Bold Feather and Nimo were of one mind. The Ancient One grasped that both of their wishes would come to be.

Nimo and Bold Feather stood apart. Their hate began to spill over onto one another with wicked glances. Bold Feather had not yet learned that Nimo was her half-sister. The Ancient One saw that Nimo would not wait much longer to tell her. Nimo's bitterness overwhelmed her good sense. She asked of herself, *Why was I not chosen? Bold Feather is also evil.*

Bold Feather was not born evil. She became evil because of her fear of abandonment. Nimo was born evil with her father's worst traits planted deeply in her heart. She glared at Bold Feather.

Bold Feather could respond only with a black shadow of warning in the depths of her eyes.

The Ancient One was attempting to stop this battle; it was to no avail.

Nimo moved to level ground and began to draw the circle of battle. Bold Feather watched with curiosity. She wondered, *Who is this woman and why does she wish to fight me? I do not know her but I will kill her for her challenge.*

The Ancient One thought, *These sisters will be evenly matched in their upcoming battle. Neither will give ground.*

The Ancient One released, without delay, Bold Feather's mind and body.

Both of these sisters were born with a huge capacity for evil and hatred along with an enormous desire for power. The evil in their souls released simultaneously and produced scarlet veils that laced across the large evening sky. Dark clouds formed above these veils to protect the very heavens from this evil. The Magic Man saw the red veils form in the sky; he felt the unleashed evil throughout his being.

Nimo grasped her spear. She ran at Bold Feather in an incomprehensible rage. She stopped short at the edge of the circle. She shouted, "You will die! I have always been in your shadow, yet I bear Geronimo's name."

Bold Feather seized her spear in an instant. She said, "What do you speak of?" as she stepped into the circle of battle.

Nimo spoke, "I have been in hiding all of my life because of you. I will not be hidden any longer. I will have the honor you have now. Your honor has left me with nothing—no pride in my ancestry, no recognition for who I am. I am Geronimo's daughter, dear sister. I have nurtured my hate for you all of my life. You never noticed me. I will kill you now!"

The battle began. Bold Feather and Nimo circled and observed one another for any obvious weaknesses that could be exploited. Nimo had the advantage; she had been nurturing her hate for a very long time. However, Bold Feather was courageous beyond most and would not fear Nimo's spear. It would not be an unfair fight.

Nimo drew first blood by attempting to cut the artery in Bold Feather's arm. Even though there was much blood, it did not stop Bold Feather. She simply waited for Nimo to come closer. This was a measure of Nimo's courage as she came closer to Bold Feather. She must or she would show fear. Bold Feather was impressed.

With no thought at all, Nimo ran at Bold Feather. Their spears intertwined. Neither would give up the advantage. Bold Feather stepped back and released her spear. She used Nimo's closeness to stab the soft skin of Nimo's breast with her spear. Bold Feather could have killed her quickly, but she was enjoying the fight. It was the sadistic evilness within her to allow her to toy with Nimo.

Bold Feather's pride was always her undoing. She was overconfident in her expertise. However, Nimo lunged unexpectedly. She positioned the point of her spear and thrust deeply into Bold Feather's abdomen.

Bold Feather knew this was a killing wound. She knew she would die. But not alone.

She leaped at Nimo and took her head off with the side of her sharp spear using the strength she had left within her spirit.

The sisters collapsed together. They held each other in death as they never would have in life. Their deaths became a certainty as they dissolved into dust upon the scarred and bloody circle of battle. Evil was destroyed and turned into nothingness. But it is true that evil leaves its mark. The scarred circle will remain always as a warning to all who would follow evil's path.

All was again as it should be. The red veil of evil had disappeared, and the clouds above had formed into a light mist to clean this evilness from the heavens. The moon was full and bright. The Ancient One of the Apaches had completed her difficult destiny.

Shining Star began to shout into the sky, "Ancient One, come into me! I must speak."

She appeared in his mind. He felt a measure of great relief that left him again in a state of puzzlement. You, I must know."

The Ancient One questioned, "Why must you know me?"

He said, "I hear your loving voice in my dreams. It is the Great Spirit's intention that I learn of you."

The Ancient One felt his sincerity deep in her heart. This sincerity was in her memories and in his eyes, his father's eyes. She was sure who he was. Her lost babe, her son, Shining Star.

She said, "May I ask your name, Great Chief?"

He said, "I am known as Shining Star."

The Ancient One said, "You have your father's eyes. You are my lost son."

Shining Star felt a ray of hope light in his heart. He has always wanted to know his mother before he died. He begged her, "Stay with me, in my mind! I do not want to lose you again."

She spoke calmly but firmly, "Son, I will see you in the Spirit World when it is your time. I have not stopped loving you, Shining Star. I crept about to listen to all of the stories told about you. My arms ached to hold you always. You were my babe. You were taken away from me by the Apache. When I held you and bestowed your birth name upon you, I sensed you were a conjurer and would always be protected by the Great Spirit. I had no fears for you."

Tears spilled over from the Great Chief's eyes. He said, "I dreamed of you, my dearest mother. I heard your voice, and I smelled your scent. I always felt closeness even though you were far away."

Shining Star continued, "Your people did not forget your birth name. You are called Gilded Rose in the old legends. It was apparent at your birth that your spirit was gold. I felt your death. Your spirit passed through me. I sensed this death was a relief for you. I begged the Great Spirit to lead you to the Spirit World, even though I sensed someone whispering to your spirit, convincing you to go to that wonderful place. I need you, Mother."

Gilded Rose spoke to her son. "Dear son, I tell you that you will be with me shortly in the Spirit World. You are ancient too. You have helped these women to become independent. It was by the will of the Great Spirit that you did these things. You have done well. I must go, my son. These two women have completed their battle.

"Remember, do not fear death, Shining Star. It is but a release. I will watch over and guide you. I love you, Shining Star. You will see my face in the Spirit World." Gilded Rose allowed him no reply; she released his mind instantly.

Shining Star could see the Great Spirit's will. His was filled with concern in sending his mother to the Spirit World with much pride. This need possessed him; it was given from the Great Spirit. He would give Gilded Rose a beautiful white-silver-gray spotted Appaloosa stallion. He was called Gray Cloud. He thought, *This unique horse will accompany her into the Spirit World. He must speak with Gray Cloud quickly. He must be willing to give his life on earth and accompany Gilded Rose.*

He whispered in Gray Cloud's ear, begging him to release his spirit and return Gilded Rose to the Spirit World. Gray Cloud's body simply collapsed upon the earth; he had chosen.

Chief Shining Star could see in his mind's eye that Gray Cloud was with Gilded Rose, standing at her side. She would be deeply honored in the Spirit World for the stunning horse and her status as the last of the faithful chosen ones. The Great Chief saw that he had done all that he could for his beloved mother.

The Great Chief Shining Star wished his mother much happiness. He hoped she had soared on the back of the beautiful Appaloosa and was instantly in the Spirit World.

The Great Chief Shining Star returned to his hut and wept great tears without shame, tears long held back for the loss of his mother. To the Apache, she would always be the Ancient One. To him, she would be his mother, Gilded Rose, with the golden spirit.

Chapter Forty-Four

Shining Star sat on his stool. It was finely crafted for a Great Chief. The covering was made of many pine needles covered with fox fur. Shining Star found it to be relaxing. He was an old man now who ached in every joint.

He was observing his people's reaction to the new women. These women were laughing together and working together, side by side. The chief thought, *Good, the new women would be accepted and loved as sisters in time.* They were certainly beautiful women. He understood the Braves' interest much better now.

As a Great Chief, Shining Star had seen that his people did not lack for the necessities of life. There was always an abundance of meat. The Braves maintained their fine hunting grounds. They took only what was needed from nature to feed the tribal members. The result was well-stocked hunting grounds. Moreover, there was no waste. Bones were boiled for their marrow, used to create needles, and for carving. Tendons were used as strips for creating sleeping furs, tunics, and moccasins. The Black Hills Tribe were prosperous. The Apache women were awed and more than willing to learn the Black Hills way.

Shining Star's mind drifted. He began to give thought to his vivid dream. In his heart, he did not doubt this was more than a vivid dream. He believed She Who Dares lay with him on that melancholy night. He remembered touching her softness and smelling her scent. Yes, she was there with him, but he asked himself, why had she never come to him before?

These thoughts led him into a frightening foretelling from the Great Spirit. It was made known to him that the Black Hills Tribe must not fade away in nothingness. This camp must move northwest for countless sunrises. The Warrior Women, the Apache women, who chose to harry the whites and to have no Brave or hearth, planned to attack and acquire the Black Hills and capture their wealth by destroying Shining Star's tribe.

Shining Star must make haste. The white man's disease will accompany them, and there will be much suffering and death. Shining Star's destiny was clear. He must relocate his people northwest. Shining Star woke from this foretelling, shouting loudly for the Medicine Man and the Magic Man.

The women became alarmed. "What has happened?" they asked one another in panic. Surely, something was amiss. They began to comfort one another with hugs and petting. They would know soon what had happened to frighten the Great Chief.

The Medicine Man and the Magic Man ran to Great Chief Shining Star. "What has happened, oh great one?" Shining Star related all that had been foretold. With sadness upon their faces, they asked, "When do we leave, Great Chief?" All Black Hills tribal members loved their home. But there was no question or doubt. The Great Spirit's love for them was the source of their happiness.

Shining Star said, "Begin the drums to bring the hunters back. We will arrange the tribunal beginning this moonrise to inform the people." He turned and walked back to his lodgings, his shoulders slumped over and his feet shuffling. His posture spoke of great grief.

The Medicine Man and the Magic Man saw that Shining Star had lost his youthful vigor. These men saw that they must help him accomplish this sorrowful task. They had every reason to believe that this was to be the last duty Shining Star would accomplish in his life. They must help persuade the people with all vigor.

The drums began. The people became frightened. The announcement was made by the Medicine Man that a tribunal would be held at moonrise. The people scurried about in dread, asking of one another what could have happened. The knowing women spoke not a word; they realized it would only upset the people further. The people walked to their lodges to wait for moonrise; they were overcome by anxiety. They were aware that the drums did not beat for insignificant reasons. This was a serious problem that would affect their lives. They could only wait until moonrise.

Chapter Forty-Five

The moon rose, displaying a brilliance not seen by the Black Hills Tribe ever before. Its message was one of impending doom. Magnificent shades of yellow among patches of intense orange swirled over its outsized face. This was the moon of calamity written of in the great prophecies. This moon was an omen. It indicated the need for an urgent departure, not only for the people, but for all of the Great Spirit's creatures. The wild animals, birds, and even the sounds of insects had disappeared from this much-loved land fated for disaster.

Shining Star's hut was disturbingly silent as he dressed. He was nearly finished. He must don his ceremonial robe that concealed his undecorated tunic and matching buckskins of finely tanned deer hide. His robe was fashioned from the fur of a massive old grizzly. He stroked the grizzly's fur and remembered with fondness the battle this great bear had given him. He began to pray; he gave his heartfelt gratitude to the bear's spirit for the gift of his impressive fur. He begged for the use of the bear's immense strength. The people must be convinced. He knew the tribunal would undergo much in this convincing.

Shining Star's hair of silver was nearly as long as his black eagle feather headdress. He worried loudly as he slipped it on his forehead. He spoke with annoyance, "Surely, the people can see and hear the signs provided by the Great Spirit. They must be amenable. It is imperative that they flee from the Warrior Women who are deadly fighters and spreaders of the white man's disease."

The white man called this disease smallpox. It was deadly and spread from one to another with very little physical contact. It caused much suffering. Pustules formed on the body and drained a greenish yellow mucus. There were high fevers and delusional thoughts. The dead and dying ones from this dreadful illness were burned. All they had touched had been thrown into the fire with them. Shining Star did not wish to have this illness in his camp.

Shining Star did think with a chuckle, *Gilded Rose taught these women too well. The Great Spirit has warned us to flee them. The Braves feel humbled. They wish to fight these Warrior Women. It is written in the great prophecies that a Brave must not fight a woman. These Braves will not disobey. It is the Black Hills way.*

Shining Star departed from his hut to see the Medicine Man and Magic Man waiting, one on each side of his hide flap. They were dressed in formal attire.

THE CHOSEN ONES

The Magic Man wore red robes designed with mysterious markings of stars, sun, and the moon of calamity painted upon the back of his robe. He bore a matching image upon his forehead. He desired that all shall perceive this glistening moon as both warning and savior to the Black Hills Tribe.

The Medicine Man wore a healing color to express harmony and peace to the people. The tunic was crafted from the hide of a spotted fawn. Drawings of ash-drawn circles symbolized the cycle of life unto death and death unto life. He wore a headdress of fawn mounted on his brow standing completely erect.

These prestigious men were carrying out their duty as Tribunal Spokespersons. The People must recognize their power and influence if they were to hear their words and be saved.

The speaking circle was placed in the center of the tribunal grounds where all the people could see and hear. All members of the Black Hills Tribe were present when these important men stepped into the circle. The people could see by their dress that this was a serious matter. They began to murmur in fear.

The Medicine Man sought to spare the Great Chief. He quieted the people and began to relate the foretelling given to the Great Chief from the Great Spirit.

The people coexisted in a state of silent horror. The people began to shout in disappointment and terror. "Must we? Can we not fight these Warrior Women? Need we leave our land and all of our belongings?"

The Magic Man stepped forward. He spoke to them kindly, as if they were children. "Do you not see the Moon of Calamity? Can you not see that the animals, birds, and the silence of insects are a sign that we must depart? This sign is from the Great Spirit. We must go at daylight on horseback. Take one spare horse and only what is needed. This camp will be burned. The Warrior Women will not be left with sanctuary."

The people began to cry and bring down curses on the heads of the Warrior Women. In their hearts, they were reluctant to leave, they were woeful, and they were angry, but they had always obeyed the Great Spirit.

Chief Shining Star stepped forward soothingly. "My dear ones, you are happy here, and you must leave. The Great Spirit would not send us where we will not be happy again. Have faith. Take only food, water, and what is necessary. The Magic Man is right, we must burn this tribal camp, and we must leave at sunrise. You must not disobey. Death will stalk those who do not listen."

Shining Star was escorted to his hut by the Medicine Man and the Magic Man. He had noticed these men hovered over him throughout the tribunal and after. He was sure they could see the wasting and weakness that had come over him these past sunrises. Even so, he must lead the people to their new home. Shining Star was given this responsibility. He had faith that the Great Spirit would not assign this duty if he would not have the strength and dignity to accomplish it.

He began to disrobe quickly in his silent hut by the light of a small fire. He lay his weakening and wasting body, concealed only in a loincloth, on his buffalo robes. Shining Star thought of the tribunal. *Sunrise will enlighten me, but I am certain the Black Hills Tribe will obey in spite of their grief, fear, and anger.*

The Black Hills Tribe was tolerating much discomfort this nightfall. Shining Star thought, *The earth is warming. It is a warning sign from the Moon of Calamity. It is far too warm in our huts. In all of my summers, I cannot recall sweltering so.* Sleep was slow in coming to all.

Nevertheless, the entire tribe was waiting at sunrise. Some faces were stoic, some were shining with tears, and some were angry. Shining Star signaled the Braves to torch the huts. He placed his back to the east while motioning with his arm for his people to follow. His heart was heavy, and his state of mind was grievous. He was a tired old man. It was time to name a successor. The choice would be difficult; all of the Braves were exemplary. His choice would be accepted. He would give this much thought as he rode northwest.

The Apache Warrior Women (Deep Waters)

The decisions we make for our own survival
are often harsh.
—Unknown

Chapter Forty-Six

Deep Waters and her tribe of Warrior Women galloped the scorching dusty trail. They were visibly armed and yapping threatening war cries. They hoped to catch the Black Hills Tribe unawares and unarmed. They were certain these gentle people would be easily overcome.

As they rounded the bend, the scent of smoke filled the air. They forced their unwilling horses to circle the camp with many strenuous kicks to the ribs. They discovered there was nothing but remnants of huts with trailing spirals of smoke floating upward.

Deep Waters whooped in anger and brandished her spear at the smoking camp. Her plan was ruined. This camp was to be their refuge. Now, nothing was left. Deep Waters rubbed the yellow streaming pustule on her cheek as she pondered what to do next. She touched her forehead in a natural response, mulling over her options. Her filthy skin was as hot as the coals in a campfire. She saw the Warrior Women could not seat their horses any longer; she saw that they had done well.

Deep Waters and her tribe of Warrior Women regretted that they had inflamed the whites with their constant attacks. They killed whole families with fire, killed their livestock with their arrows, and poisoned their wells. Now, in retaliation, the whites sent a large posse of white men to pursue them and kill them.

These women were lean and hard. They had been taken for Braves by the attacked whites. This could have been the Warrior Women's escape from the white posse. The whites would not suspect a camp of diseased, starving, helpless women as their attackers. They would ride past this clever disguise.

Deep Waters' illness did not allow her to see this chance at escape. Her heart seethed with revenge and hate. Deep Waters did perceive that her tribe would be killed or imprisoned if captured. Neither of these consequences appealed to her. Her solution, arising from the condition of her heart, was they must fight these white men. Without warning, she could not recall why they were fleeing the whites.

The Medicine Woman, spoken of as Jasmine, reminded her that the whites carried rifles. Jasmine was beautiful in spite of her leanness. Her raven hair complemented her lips and perfectly shaped face. Her lips were the color of wild cherry trees blooming in the spring. She wore the robe and headdress portraying her status as Medicine Woman. The robe was crafted from the hide of an old cow buffalo. This kill was a daring feat that flaunted her great bravery. Her headdress was created from the feathers of a circling hawk shot down from the skies above her. Again, she flaunted her skill with the bow and arrow. It was the way of the Warrior Women tribe.

It appeared as if she was the only uninfected Warrior Woman. Jasmine thought, *The tribe of Warrior Women are facing death from illness and from the swiftly approaching white men armed with rifles. I must offer them up to the whites to save myself. I must remove my war paint, hide my weapons, and carry a flag of surrender. Surely, the whites would not shoot me.* She soon realized that she would be placed in the white man's prison simply because of her red skin. The traitorous act she would perform for these white men would mean nothing to them.

An idea occurred to her as she agonized in her mind for a way to save her life, a life of freedom. She thought, *I have no loyalty in my heart for Deep Waters. I must slip away and follow the trail of the Black Hills Tribe.* It would not be known she had ridden with the Warrior Women; she would not tell them.

Jasmine was unaware that she was in the early stages of the white man's disease. Her illness did not allow her to remember the Apache women who became mates to the Black Hills Braves. It did not come to her that they would recognize her. She could only visualize a welcome from the tribe. She thought feverishly, *Yes, this is a much better idea. I will creep away when night falls.*

Jasmine had yet to notice her skin burning during sunlight or her coldness at nightfall. She would have been horrified to learn she was not immune as she believed. Her precautions had not protected her. She would develop the fever and the pustules soon. It would drive her to desperately pursue the trail of the Black Hills Tribe. Her mind would continue to imagine that these people would provide health, safety, and security.

However, the outcome would be far different.

Chapter Forty-Seven

The whites were coming. Hoofbeats could be heard loudly.

Deep Waters ordered, "Women, apply heavy war paint to the hands and face quickly."

The women complied without knowing the reason for this command. All knew that their Great Chief was not to be questioned.

The whites were suddenly upon them. The women rallied with their arrows in spite of their great weakness. They had no chance, but they fought until their end as the rifles took them, one by one.

Deep Waters was forcibly separated from the Warrior Women; she had been recognized as the chief of this tribe. She whooped eccentrically as they charged her. She fought them with the strength of a mad animal. She forced them to touch her burning skin. Deep Waters thought gleefully, *These whites will soon die.*

She was overcome by the whites and tied to a tree for execution. She was baited by this posse of angry white men. Deep Waters refused in silence to beg for her life. She could see there was nothing left to beg for; she was dying with the white man's disease. She remained silent on the outside. In her diseased mind, she begged the Great Spirit for revenge above all. She also begged for faith, courage, endurance, and to die bravely. Her silence enticed them to shoot her in non-vital areas. She did not weep or cry out, even though her body jerked involuntarily. The loss of her life-giving blood brought an end to her life. She and her tribe died bravely. By their faith alone, they found their way to the Spirit World. Deep Waters' plans for revenge did not fail. She would soon see the finish.

In disbelief, the white posse examined the dead bodies in a riffraff slovenly fashion and saw that they had killed women. They said to one another with pride, "These'uns must be the Warrior Women Tribe. They been heard about 'cross the state of Texas. Ain't it grand? Us volunteers shot up the Warrior Women Tribe. Yee-haw!" They shouted blasphemies that smacked of smugness and slapped each other's backs in triumph. They grinned hugely at what they considered an accomplishment. Jubilation flooded their features.

One said, "Shouldn't we look over these squaws for valuables? Who can tell with Injuns? I guess we ought to burn 'em too."

They would soon learn that Deep Waters would have her revenge. The posse noticed the signs of smallpox hidden beneath war paint carefully smeared heavily upon the Warrior Women's faces.

Their cries of triumph ceased immediately. It was sheer panic that prevented the whites from burning the diseased bodies. They fled swiftly, and the smallpox fled with them as a weight upon their shoulders. They could hear the echo of Deep Waters' whooping following them as they galloped away.

In their panic, this volunteer posse returned to their settlement. They approached waving a white flag. A messenger was sent to them. He remained a long distance away, but within hollering distance. He listened to their accounting, reassured them all would be well, and rode away.

This gleeful and triumphant posse was shot to death and their bodies burned by their own settlement.

Deep Waters watched triumphantly from the Spirit World.

Chapter Forty-Eight

Jasmine slipped away as she had planned. She was following the trail of the Black Hills Tribe with all haste. She would reach them soon. She could read much in their tracks. They traveled slowly. They tugged a spare horse behind them. Jasmine thought, *Why must they tug a spare horse along? Is this wise of the Great Chief?* She felt so hot. She gazed at the sun and swore angrily.

She halted at sunrise, wiping the sweat from her brow. Her exposed forearm revealed to her a small puffy red rash. She quickly examined her body's trunk. The rash was plentiful throughout the length of her abdomen.

She shrieked out of anger and a wild denial. "It cannot be! I took many precautions. It is only a rash from the extreme heat and the dampness that follows! I will not be sick with the white man's disease!"

Her denials did not change the truth; she had seen many sick Warrior Women. Her line of thought continued. *I must find my way to the Great Chief Shining Star quickly. They are a gentle people. They will take me in, heal this illness, and I may live. I must hurry.*

Jasmine's mind was obsessed. If she could have reasoned, she would have understood that this was not likely to take place. The white man and the red man feared this deadly disease. Shining Star would not be out of the ordinary. His sympathy would not overrule his responsibility. He must protect his tribe. Shining Star would never allow her to approach his people. The obsession she nurtured would be the cause of her death.

It was not long before she became much more feverish. She could not reason at all, and her memories were lost to her. She doggedly followed the Black Hills Tribe as the pustules erupted and drained. She only thought of saving her life.

Jasmine grasped her horse's mane and allowed it to follow the trail. The horse stopped when the trail stopped. It was a stunning golden sunrise. The heat caused her to shine with dampness and to scratch her draining pustules.

Jasmine placed herself under a flag of truce, knowing they would not accept her otherwise. She was still obsessed and still believed the Black Hills Tribe would take her in and heal her. She saw the scouts riding up the rise to report her presence and location. She whispered with her weak, raspy voice, "Soon. It will be soon now."

The Great Chief Shining Star rode out with the Medicine Man and the Magic Man to observe the woman who should dare to approach his tribe. She waved her flag desperately. This action told Shining Star that she was also desperate.

The Medicine Man spoke sorrowfully. "This lone woman has the white man's disease. She brings great danger to our tribe. She must be slain and her body burned."

The Magic Man felt no sympathy for this lone woman. He said, "She seeks to hide the truth from our tribe. She is a traitorous renegade belonging to the Warrior Women's tribe. She must perish for this reason alone."

The Great Chief reached behind him and drew an arrow. He motioned for the Magic Man to set the arrow afire. Shining Star positioned the flaming arrow and released the twine.

Jasmine saw the flaming arrow and turned to flee. The flaming arrow arced through the sky and planted itself firmly in Jasmine's lower spine. She fell to the ground and curled her upper body into itself in an attempt to evade the fire. She screamed horribly as the magical fire enveloped her. Her screams did not stop until she was lifeless and her body was burned to ashes.

The Great Chief Shining Star observed, "The decisions we make for our own survival are often harsh."

THE ARAPAHOE TRIBE

(GREAT CHIEF BLACK KETTLE)

The Great Spirit is merciful to all of
his people. It is often forgotten.
—Unknown

Chapter Forty-Nine

The Black Hills Tribe traveled northwest, sunrise after sunrise, as their Great Chief had foretold. Their trail led them into the foothills of a whole host of mountains. These mountains joined together and split away from each other to bring into being many other mountains. The summits could be seen in the distance. It brought the people an overwhelming sense of awe. They could not help but gawk at the most beautiful and largest mountain in this land located far to the north. This mountain was the color of periwinkles and capped with winter's snow throughout the high summer. The people despaired. Would the Great Spirit lead them in their quest to climb this majestic mountain? They prayed fervently, time and again, for the finding of a new home.

Shining Star was growing weaker with each sunrise. He thought, *I must be the one to complete this destiny. The Great Spirit will guard my well-being until the people are settled in our new habitat.* His musing was invaded by the scent of dampness permeating the air.

He prayed, "Please, Great Spirit, show your servant that we have reached the end of our journey. The people are driven to the end of their endurance. I am an old one and weary. Please bring us to this flowing river. Let it be the end of our journey."

An uphill trail brought them to a lovely river that boasted a small waterfall. The people waited quietly and remained mounted while the Braves scouted the surrounding land. On their return, they reported to Shining Star that this land was isolated of settlements, it was suitable for huts and gardens, and the tracks of abundant game were seen in the surrounding forest. The people looked intently at Shining Star, hope in their eyes.

Shining Star was conscious of the Great Spirit's passage through his soul. He was also aware of a tribe of many Braves riding quickly from the south from whence they came.

The Great Chief was in the lead. He wore on his shoulders the head and fur of a cougar. His headdress was an unadorned rawhide band woven with many eagle feathers. He wore only an unembellished deer skin tunic. He was followed by the Medicine Man and the Magic Man. They each wore deer skin tunics and eagle feather headdresses, as if they wished to show their unity with their chief. They brought many armed Braves. The Braves carried their bows and arrows in plain sight.

Shining Star's heart fell. He thought, *We will all be massacred. There is no time to prepare for battle.* He felt his faith return to him. His fear dissolved into a feeling of calmness. He prayed loudly, "Please, Great Spirit, allow this formidable tribe to see that we are no threat to their land."

Shining Star commanded, "Scouts, lower your bows. All is well."

The Great Chief halted within hollering distance. Shining Star could see his bravery in this act; he was within arrowshot.

This Great Chief spoke loudly, "We have watched you for many sunrises. It has come to our ears that you are the homeless tribe from the far south. I am called Great Chief Black Kettle of the Arapahoe Tribe. We are a peaceful tribe. We are armed for protection if we should be attacked by your tribe. We will not attack your tribe without provocation."

Shining Star spoke loudly, "Great Chief Black Kettle. I am the Great Chief Shining Star. My people and I are the homeless ones you speak of. The Tribe of Warrior Women intended to attack us and use our camp for their refuge. These women carried the white man's disease. We burned our camp to leave them without refuge. We could not fight them. We must not fight women. It is forbidden in our great prophecies."

Shining Star continued, "The Great Spirit has led us to this beautiful place. We wish to settle here with your benevolent permission."

The Medicine Man belonging to the Arapahoe tribe spoke suddenly and without provocation. "Great Chief Shining Star is nearing the Spirit World."

Chief Black Kettle asked, "Have you chosen a successor, Chief Shining Star?"

Chief Shining Star answered, "I have, Chief Black Kettle. This announcement will be made at moonrise."

Chief Black Kettle stated bluntly, "Your name, Chief Shining Star, has come to my ears. You are spoken of as a wise chief. You understand that I must know of the chosen successor in order to make this decision you ask of me. He must come forward and allow the Medicine Man and the Magic Man to see his heart."

Chief Shining Star said, "I do understand that you as a Great Chief must meet my successor. However, he does not know I have chosen him."

Chief Black Kettle said, "That is for the best. We will ride forward, and you will present him to us. He will soon know."

Chief Shining Star did not question Great Chief Black Kettle. It was usual that Shining Star choose the successor with the agreement of his Medicine Man and Magic Man. This agreement must be set aside. Chief Shining Star was searching for land for his people.

Shining Star shouted, "Storm Bear, approach us."

Storm Bear was startled, yet he obeyed. He fell to his knees in front of Shining Star and said, "I am not worthy, Great Chief."

Shining Star said, "I have observed you long, Storm Bear. You are worthy."

Black Kettle's holy men examined Storm Bear closely.

The Medicine Man spoke, "I see no fault in him."

The Magic Man spoke, "He is peace loving, kind, and fair. He is an excellent choice for a Great Chief."

The Medicine Man spoke, "Chief Shining Star will be taken to the Spirit World soon. He must make the announcement to the Black Hills Tribe that Storm Bear is the Great Chief upon his death. It is necessary to leave no doubts in the people's mind."

Chief Black Kettle asked, "Do you fear dying, Chief Shining Star?"

Chief Shining Star cried out, "I wish it, Chief Black Kettle. My escort to the Spirit World is my beloved. I only fear for the fate of my people."

Chief Black Kettle smiled. "Your People are as safe as we are. The white man sees only red and white. You are fortunate to have passed by them without their knowledge." Chief Black Kettle stated, "We must have the adoption ceremony. We must be brothers before we become neighbors. You and your homeless ones will become Arapahoe. We are known as fierce fighters. The white man will fear you."

He extended an exposed forearm. The Medicine Man slashed it. Chief Shining Star and Storm Bear lifted their arms. Their arms were held tightly together by Black Kettle's Medicine Man, allowing their Black Hills blood and the Arapahoe's blood to mingle.

Chief Black Kettle said, "Your people and my people have become brothers. Build your camp, Chief Storm Bear, on this land called Colorado. We will meet again, brothers." He raised his hand, reared his horse, and departed south with all haste.

Shining Star announced loudly to the people, "The Great Spirit has led you to this new camp."

The people yipped and yapped, displaying their extreme happiness.

Shining Star sat his horse patiently as he waited for the people to quiet. He said, "You will now be known as the Arapahoe Tribe. You must always be their brothers and remain peaceful with their wishes. They have given you this land."

His People nodded their heads in solemn agreement. All would be as Shining Star wished.

Shining Star's weakness required him to rest on his stool. He silently thanked the Great Spirit for this wonderful land and their newly found brothers. He watched the new Arapahoe Tribe behave as children; they were overflowing with excitement. Shining Star waited for them to unload their horses and take them to water. Once the horses were watered, they began to jump in the clear cold river fully clothed. They laughed as they felt the cold. They began splashing one another as small children. Shining Star had never seen them so happy or so playful. His eyes were drawn to the soon-to-be Great Chief Storm Bear. The people approached him respectfully. Most of them remembered he was born on a wild, dark, stormy night. He was a huge babe for the birthing. All fretted in fear for his mother. She survived the birth of such a bear of a babe, and he grew to be a bear of a man.

THE CHOSEN ONES

Storm Bear scooped up many children and tossed them into the river, but not without a watchful eye. His heart was thoughtful and caring. He was respectful to the old and kind to all the people. Shining Star felt blessed that the Great Spirit allowed him to see his successor's good heart.

There was still much to do. But these tasks would be done by Storm Bear. Shining Star's mind began to drift as old ones do. He thought, *There is time to build huts once tools are crafted. The huts must withstand heavy snow and wild hungry animals. There would be the stocking of the huts holding wild game. Much wood must be stock-piled for warmness. Warm clothing and moccasins must be crafted from the hides of successful hunts. The women must learn to make this clothing with thickness and warmth. Severe weather would come early. They must be ready. Storm Bear would see what needed to be done for the people. There would be much for him to learn.* Shining Star stopped himself from fretting. The Great Spirit would be with them all.

He must have a formal ceremony appointing Storm Bear as his successor at moonrise. The Medicine Man and the Magic Man will approve Storm Bear as a formality. Shining Star chuckled. No doubt, these intuitive holy men had intended to suggest that Storm Bear be named successor. They had always known his mind long before him.

The Great Chief Shining Star thought, *My destiny is fulfilled.* He felt enthusiastic; he would see his only wife, She Who Dares, and his mother, Gilded Rose, very soon now.

Chapter Fifty

The moon was rising. Living in the mountains transported the heavens nearer to man's eye. It was all but time for the ceremony. Shining Star wore his finery as Great Chief to show his respect for Storm Bear. The people must be aware of the honor due to Storm Bear and his appointment as successor. The moon had nearly completed its rise into a darkening sky sparkling with stars.

The Medicine Man and the Magic Man appeared to assist Shining Star. He could not walk without assistance. The stump of a fallen oak tree had been placed in the center of the speaking circle. The people saw their Great Chief's weakness as he sat on the stump. Their faces were solemn, stunned, and wet with tears.

They whispered quietly among themselves, "Chief Shining Star has become weak and helpless. He will leave us soon for the Spirit World. Even though he is nearly lifeless, he does this last duty with pride. Storm Bear is to be appointed to fill his great moccasins."

THE CHOSEN ONES

The Medicine Man and the Magic Man stepped forward, one on each side of Chief Shining Star. They intended to spare the Great Chief and save his strength.

The Magic Man shouted, "We meet here tonight to name a successor for our beloved Great Chief Shining Star. We concur with his choice of the loyal and affectionate Storm Bear. It is requested that he be given the people's respect and obedience. Does anyone object to Shining Star's choice?"

No one cried out in dissent.

Shining Star spoke, "It is my wish that the adopted Arapahoe Tribe accept Storm Bear with their whole heart. You must comply with his wishes in spite of any differences between you. This is a serious matter, my people. Do you agree to accept Storm Bear? If you do not, the punishment will be exile. This is my last command as Great Chief."

All of the people cried out, "Storm Bear, Storm Bear, Great Chief Storm Bear!"

Chief Shining Star said, "Thank you, my people. You are dismissed now."

As Shining Star's people departed, his thoughts fluctuated between the present and the past as old ones often do. He thought with serious-minded bewilderment, *My body has become weary and ancient, yet my spirit remains young at heart. I do not feel as an old one until I must complete the simplest task. I do recall and grieve for my lost and carefree youth. I could not imagine at that time that I would ever become an old one. I guffawed gleefully at the warnings I received from my brothers.*

His thoughts continued. *My body wastes away. I do wonder how I have not thoroughly understood that death must happen to all living creatures. I see the death of man as a waste of wisdom, knowledge, and skill. It is a waste to live and achieve.*

He continued to search intensely in his mind for the understanding he needed. He believed the circle of life and death existed. But why must a man die?

He spoke silently and harshly within his mind. *This is only fear, Shining Star. These are an old one's musings borne out of terror from my state of near death.* He recognized his terror, and the answer became clear. The purpose of a harsh life is to bring compassion for the suffering of others. Fear of death comes for the reason that a man lacks the ability to comprehend the state of death; man fears what he does not know. Gilded Rose cautioned him long ago, "Do not fear death, my son."

Oh, shush yourself Shining Star. Focus on the Spirit World. All things are made right there. Shining Star overcame his fear. He had accepted that all things that live must die.

CHAPTER FIFTY-ONE

Noises came to Shining Star's ears. He could perceive that these noises were expressions of awe, happiness, and a blend of humility.

Shining Star wished to know why the people were expressing themselves in this manner. He called for the Medicine Man and the Magic Man. They did not come. He was unable to stand alone, so he must trust that they would come. Shining Star thought, *The Medicine Man and the Magic Man are attempting to calm the people. But from what? Bring peace to yourself, Shining Star. All will be well.*

A magnificent gray-spotted and luminous Appaloosa stallion walked slowly through the camp. His hoofs struck sparks from the rocky trail. He bore double; women led by an impressive Chief dressed in all his finery.

An old one cried out gleefully, "It is the Great Chief Geronimo. He glows as one from the Spirit World. Show respect for the Great Spirit's mercy!"

The people fell to their knees and bowed their heads. Tears flowed from their eyes.

The Medicine Man and the Magic Man arrived. They must instruct the people.

Each spoke in turn. "The Great Chief Geronimo brings the mother of Shining Star, who is called Gilded Rose, and his beloved who is called She Who Dares. The old ones will recall. They are sent from the Spirit World to lead the spirit of the Great Chief Shining Star to the Spirit World. The adopted Arapahoe Tribe has been blessed by their obedience. The Great Spirit has allowed you to see Shining Star's flight. You may follow quietly."

The Medicine Man and the Magic Man sprinted in haste to Shining Star. They had left him sitting on the oak stump in the speaking circle. They heard his call to them, but they could not leave the panicked people. The Medicine Man and the Magic Man were also old ones. They had been with Shining Star since he wore the headdress of a Great Chief. They were winded when they arrived. In their weakness, they could not speak or raise him up as his dignity would demand for this ordeal.

The Spirit Ones approached rapidly; Shining Star was taken unawares. She Who Dares stepped into the speaking circle. Shining Star was astounded that he should receive such favor in the eyes of the Great Spirit.

He thought, *She is so beautiful. Her spirit blazes as bright as the stars above me.*

She responded to him, "Much gratitude for your thoughts, husband."

Gilded Rose stepped into the speaking circle. Shining Star saw that she was young and very beautiful. He spoke, "My mother and my wife have come for me. I am blessed."

Gilded Rose spoke, "My faithful son, the Great Spirit thinks highly of you. You were tested and overcame the fear of death through much soul-searching. I gift you with the Appaloosa called Gray Cloud. You gifted me with him, and I return him. He must bear this Great Chief, Shining Star, and his beloved, She Who Dares, into the Spirit World. He is fit for a Great Chief. I must return as the Great Spirit wishes and await you, my son." She became a golden light.

Shining Star was given another great gift. His son, Geronimo, stepped into the speaking circle leading the Appaloosa.

Shining Star cried out in relief, "Oh, my beloved son! I have prayed for your spirit each night. I am overwhelmed. My tears flow freely. I can only express my gratitude and thankfulness with inadequate words to the Great Spirit. He has been merciful. My heart throbs with happiness."

Geronimo said, "I have much gratitude for your prayers, my honorable father. I have missed you and wished many times for your wise counsel. I must go, Father. I will await you by remaining with Gilded

Rose." His spirit simply disappeared. This brought tears to Shining Star's eyes.

She Who Dares raised her hand to Shining Star. She said, "The choice is yours, my husband. You may return with me, or you may live out the rest of your days. This decision will not matter. You have achieved the Spirit World."

Shining Star said, "My dear wife, I cannot let you go. You are my beloved, my true love throughout my long life. I long to hold you close and kiss your honeyed lips. I can feel your long, smooth, fine hair sliding through my fingers. I have dreamt that I lay with you. Upon waking, I could smell your fresh scent upon my bare chest. Our love extends into the Spirit World just as the Great Spirit loves his creatures. You are the greatest blessing I have received this moonrise. I love you, She Who Dares. It began when I saw you fight for your child's life. Who could not love a woman with the courage of an enraged buffalo?" Shining Star raised up his hand without fear.

She Who Dares, with great relief, grasped his hand. She had wished for this.

He transformed before the people's eyes. His body was old and lifeless, but his spirit rose. He was a young man. The people were privileged to see Shining Star blaze as She Who Dares. She led him to the impressive Appaloosa. Gray Cloud lifted them up and up, out of the people's sight.

It is so. Their love will never end.

GREAT CHIEF STORM BEAR

Acceptance of defeat while
continuing the effort to win
is the definition of a Great Chief.
—Unknown

CHAPTER FIFTY-TWO

Storm Bear gently cradled Shining Star's aged silver and lifeless skull within his enormous hands. He pressed this beloved head tightly against his own dripping cheek. Storm Bear's tears were huge, plentiful, and were a demonstration to the people of Storm Bear's heartfelt feelings. They watched his gleaming tears coat Shining Star's lifeless face.

The people could only reason as they had been taught. Had not Storm Bear been privileged to witness Shining Star's assent as he came to be one with the Spirit World? They questioned, each one to their selves, "Why does Storm Bear weep as one heartbroken?"

Their cultural beliefs taught that deep grief was not appropriate for one who has risen to the Spirit World. They began to fear Storm Bear's ability to be the Great Chief. The people began to shuffle their feet and murmur in confusion. They felt awkward, fearful, and disloyal. These feelings sharpened their perceptiveness. However, the intervention and the discernment of the Great Spirit did not allow them to sense Storm Bear's terror.

Storm Bear was simply not ready to lose Shining Star or his great wisdom. The loss of Shining Star's knowledge was overwhelming and caused Storm Bear to feel that his life was overwhelming, even though he was the first Dream Weaver in many turns of the sun.

The old ones were privileged by the Great Spirit to see and feel Storm Bear's need. These ones vowed in their hearts to provide any aid Storm Bear would request of them. The old ones saw, even though he was a very young man, nearly a youth, that Storm Bear's heart allowed Shining Star's selection for the next Great Chief. These ones could see within their heart that Shining Star had chosen wisely in Storm Bear. The old ones knew that the death of a living thing, loved and cherished, brings grief. Grief, once absorbed into the heart, brings despondency so harsh that it touches the depths of a man's bone. However, despondency soon becomes a weight far too heavy to bear. It must be thrown from the heart out of necessity. The old ones were confident this time would come for Storm Bear. They saw that his Dream Weaver powers would bring this about. He would soon understand he must not allow his grief to rule his heart. He must thrust this deep feeling of despondency from him. The old ones were patient.

The people were a different worry. They could not understand that Storm Bear's grief was necessary. Its intensity allowed his heart to speak to his soul. He could see his paralyzing fear was brought about by loneliness and a feeling of helplessness.

Storm Bear had always been an onlooker and not a participant. He gained much knowledge and patience that were far beyond his years. Shining Star saw these qualities. Therefore, he chose Storm Bear to be his successor.

Storm Bear's newly gained status generated no hidden kernel of delight in his heart. His overwhelming grief forced Storm Bear to awareness. He saw his lack of confidence in stepping into Great Chief Shining Star's moccasins. His Dream Weaver wisdom spoke to him; he must rise to his responsibilities, or Shining Star's death would be worth nothing.

Storm Bear wiped his dripping swollen eyes. He gazed about with curiosity. The people's eyes expressed a deep fear. Storm Bear understood and believed as they did; he must lack the wisdom to lead this newly adopted Arapahoe Tribe. His grief had made it evident to the people that he could not fulfill the responsibility and trust Shining Star had placed upon his spirit. His heart felt an expanding terror; it undid the small of amount of courage he now possessed. He became ashamed of his cowardice, and this brought fresh tears from his eyes. Storm Bear could see plainly that he must stop weeping if only for the sake of the people. Storm Bear's Dream Weaver's wisdom brought to Storm Bear's mind that this necessity was one more uncontrollable and demanding act of survival. He must cast away despondency and allow a gentle sadness to enter his spirit. This gentle sadness was not unlike the descent of a new spring rain. It refreshed the whole of our soul while giving rise to experience and wisdom. Loss is borne, and survival is accomplished. Storm Bear could see this plainly; it is the way of a man's life. He viewed himself with disgust. Was he a papoose needing the comforting embrace of his mother?

Shining Star saw Storm Bear's grief from the Spirit World and felt a deep pity. He spoke to this lonely, panicked, and grieving soul, "Storm Bear, you must rely on the Great Spirit. Yes, it is foretold that you will fail, but you will not fail from lack of courage.

"You must fear no more. I have chosen well and wisely with the Great Spirit's guidance. You are worthy. Your name is written in the stars. Your powers will do much good and bring happiness to the people. The Great Spirit awaits each of us simply for our goodness of heart and the gentleness of our spirit. You must go forth and become a Great Chief."

Chapter Fifty-Three

Shining Star's prophetic foretelling was not without purpose. As with Gilded Rose, his duty must continue from within the Spirit World. He must bring peace to Storm Bear's tumultuous heart. Shining Star could see that a large portion of Storm Bear's grief came from the loss of one who loved him. Storm Bear craved love, but due to his solitary nature, he lacked love. Shining Star saw that he must touch Storm Bear's gentle nature.

He spoke, "Storm Bear, I chose you for your gentleness of spirit. The people will approach you. In their hand will be trust and love. Their woes, they will bring to you, knowing with confidence a fair solution. They will not fear your temper, yet you must show no fear." Shining Star sought to reach Storm Bear's spirit. He said, "Your strength and courage will become known among many tribes."

Storm Bear heard Shining Star's prophetic wisdom. He saw clearly that he must lay aside his despondency and care for his people. Storm Bear lay his beloved great chief gently upon the oak stump that supported his body. His tears flowed no more. Yet he could not refrain from examining Shining Star's withered, lifeless body. He concluded that departure from this world was a loss of wisdom. A man's thoughts, strength, and power deteriorated into this state of uselessness. He was unaware that these thoughts belong to all men. He was only aware that he was melancholy. Storm Bear thought, *Should a man achieve to the best of his ability when this is his reward?*

Shining Star once again spoke within his mind. "Hear me, Storm Bear, I see no waste. Death is a natural result of all living beings. Death is proof of the endurance necessary for survival. A life of toil has ended. You must see it as recompense. You have forgotten the Spirit World."

Shining Star continued, "Storm Bear, you must rule the people with no self-indulgence and with the guidance of the Great Spirit. You must lend your ear with respect to the old ones. They will guide you well. Their wisdom is abundant. Heed me, Storm Bear. A Great Chief discerns that one's life is not akin to another's. All men must walk alone, through life and death, yet all must be subject to the will of the Great Spirit."

Storm Bear was resigned. He was Great Chief Storm Bear. Shining Star's words left him with no doubts.

He stood, dignified and towering with his great height. He faced the people. His facial expression was one of dutifulness—the dutifulness of a Great Chief. Storm Bear saw the high opinion of the people return to him. He felt hot courage flow throughout his backbone as his grief dissipated; the Great Spirit was with him. It was time to see to the body of Shining Star.

Storm Bear began the arrangements to see to the disposal of Shining Star's body. He spoke, "My people, a glorious funeral pyre must be built. It is well known that a Great Chief owns nothing but his attire and the articles earned from his victorious acts of bravery. All things necessary for Shining Star's use in the Spirit World must be placed within his pyre. Display your love for Shining Star with your generosity, my people. Shining Star's spirit must take to the skies at sunrise."

Storm Bear's people gathered long before sunrise. Each had labored from moonrise to sunrise in order to build the awe-inspiring, tremendous pyre. It rested on immense logs, which had been cut and rolled from the forest. The women lined these logs with the most beautiful and fragrant brush found among the undergrowth within the forest.

Shining Star's body lay in splendor. He was dressed in his ancient grizzly bear robe covering his soft deerskin tunic. His black eagle feather headdress lay on either side of his majestic face. His long silver hair had been brushed so thoroughly that it shone. Shining Star's pyre was surrounded among many necessities for his use in the spirit world. The people had been generous.

Storm Bear was pleased. He thought, *My Great Chief will not want in the Spirit World.* He was then startled out of his musings.

A loud voice shouted in his mind, "Get on with it, Storm Bear! I grow inpatient. I do not wish for my spirit to be tied to my body any longer!"

Storm Bear did not hesitate. He signaled the archers to shoot their flaming arrows. Shining Star's pyre was unexpectedly engulfed in flames with a thunderous whoosh. The intense heat forced the people to step far back. All were witnesses as Shining Star's ashes of silver separated from the gray ashes of logs and fragrant brush. The wind came up with no warning. It carried silver ashes upward and into the heavens. Shining Star was free.

Chapter Fifty-Four

During Storm Bear's wee-hour reflections, he heard in his mind the words of Shining Star: "Lend your ear to the old ones." Storm Bear embraced Shining Star's aged Medicine Man and Magic Man. He also began to seek out wisdom from the old ones to begin preparations for winter. These old ones were willing, and they were modestly flattered.

Storm Bear did not recognize that these actions of his were a kind of wisdom belonging only to himself. The old ones could see. They knew that all men reveal their humility, or their lack of humility, when it is necessary to ask others for aid. Storm Bear was humble and respectful. The old ones gave their knowledge freely. They wanted this Great Chief to succeed.

They had not heard Shining Star's prophecy. It was spoken into Storm Bear's ears as he wept throughout Shining Star's death. Shining Star had prophesied that Storm Bear would fail, but not from a lack of courage. Yet the Great Spirit had judged him and found him worthy as one who would ascend into the Spirit World. Storm Bear had meditated on this prophecy. He came to realize that his failure would be out of his control. He must take care of his people during the time remaining to him. He could not fall into melancholy. He saw that he was given a destiny to fulfill. He determined that he would remain as one worthy of the Spirit World. This determination would remain with him throughout his life.

Storm Bear soon realized that living in these mountains was very different from his homeland. These mountains were called the Rocky Mountains by the Arapahoe. Many Arapahoe customs began from their life experiences in this cruel climate. Storm Bear saw that he and his people had much to learn and a short time to learn these Arapahoe customs that would bring them survival.

The cool air was only a warning of what was to come. It brought a distinct nip to Storm Bear's shivering body on this shady sunrise. Storm Bear observed that his people were sleeping on fall leaves that peppered the ground. Others were curled up close to the belly of their mounts. Storm Bear's anxiety was nearly overwhelming. He had a great fear that their arrival was far too late for these northern climes. There were huts to build, meat to hunt, and firewood to cut and store. The women must tan hides and sew many pieces of warm clothing. Storm Bear prayed with fear in his heart, "Oh Great Spirit, there is so much to do before the harsh cold and the blizzards arrive. Please help me to accomplish these tasks. You have given me the responsibility to care for the people. Your people need your blessings, Great Spirit. I am but an ignorant man. I have searched my dreams. My dream weaver powers have left me. I can only see a suffocating blackness in my dreams. It is my destiny to die with courage. In spite of the death that awaits, I must save your people."

The Great Spirit did hear Storm Bear's prayer.

An idea occurred to Storm Bear. He concluded that he needed to speak to the Arapahoe for knowledge and assistance. They were his blood brothers. They would guide him. He left for the Arapahoe settlement as the sunrise topped the trees.

He was aware that he must emulate the Arapahoe. They were familiar with the nature of the Rocky Mountains and knew how to use this nature for their benefit. The Arapahoe wore knee-high moccasins. Waterproofing was applied using the sticky sap from the surrounding pine trees. Even though Storm Bear's mind was cluttered with anxieties, it did allow him to admire this clever idea. He hoped his Arapahoe brothers would help him to do all the necessary things for the people's survival. His fretfulness spurred him onward as he rode to the Arapahoe camp.

Shining Star watched from the Spirit World. He saw that Storm Bear would succeed in nearly all the tasks belonging to a Great Chief. However, the climes of a harsh winter would not allow Storm Bear to succeed. Storm Bear would see and attempt to remedy this lack. His actions would bring about his death. He would die with all courage as a Great Chief. Shining

Star saw he would fulfill his destiny upon his untimely death. Shining Star had always known all was in the hands of the Great Spirit. Storm Bear would be seen to; there was no reason for worry. He must only wait and welcome Storm Bear to the Spirit World.

Chapter Fifty-Five

As Storm Bear approached the Arapahoe camp, he was challenged by the Braves. He begged the Braves to ask for an audience with Great Chief Black Kettle. Word was sent to the Great Chief, and the audience was granted.

Storm Bear approached the Arapahoe Great Chief Black Kettle with his head lowered. He allowed the humbleness in his heart to be evident to this Great Chief.

The Magic Man spoke, "He is here to beg our aid for the benefit of his people. Storm Bear is blessed with a humble character. This is no ruse. It is an honest characteristic brought to him by his dream weaver's powers, oh Great One."

The Medicine Man spoke, "Oh Great Chief, we have many buffalo skins. His women have great skill in the creation of many items needed to survive the Colorado winter." The Medicine Man continued to plead on Storm Bear's behalf. "Can we not help them build their lodges and get much meat stored? They are our adopted brothers. They are Arapahoe."

Storm Bear bowed his head as he spoke to Chief Black Kettle, "Please, oh Great One, I have come to beg assistance from my Arapahoe brothers. We have arrived in this country much too late. Yet I must care for my people. We are without tools to build lodges. We have no axes to stock firewood, we must store much meat, and we have no hides for the women to create warm clothes. We lack all that is necessary to survive this harsh and long winter coming upon us. We will surely perish. Will our Arapahoe brothers support their adopted tribe in surviving this mighty winter? My people and I will be grateful to the powerful Arapahoe Tribe for the knowledge and aid received by your blood brothers."

Great Chief Black Kettle spoke from his large heart, "Your words have made me feel a great fondness for you, Storm Bear. You have displayed your blamelessness and your wisdom by approaching us. Shining Star chose his successor wisely." He turned and continued, "Medicine Man and Magic Man, preparations must be made. You must bring all of the Braves except for the ones who must stay to guard the camp. The rest of the camp must go. We will bring tools and our great hunters. This responsibility I give to you. You must not fail. The Arapahoe people cannot leave our adopted brothers to die. Sleep well, Storm Bear. We Arapahoe will arrive shortly after the next sun's rising."

Great Chief Black Kettle received a foretelling. All of the feats required to save the adopted Arapahoe Tribe were for naught. It would simply prolong the inevitably of Storm Bear's failure. However, it was the Great Spirit's wish, and the Arapahoe Tribe did hear the Great Spirit's words. Storm Bear would fail, yet he had a special place awaiting him in the Spirit World. In spite of his failure, he had heart, much love, reliability, humbleness, and intelligence. He was a chosen one of the Great Spirit.

The Great Chief Black Kettle heard and obeyed.

* * *

The sound of horse-drawn travois could be heard before the sun completed its rise into the lavender sky. The people leapt from their makeshift sleeping robes. Excitement dominated their sleep-saturated faces.

They whispered to one another, "Storm Bear has succeeded in his quest. He has brought rescue from the Great Chief of the Arapahoe. Storm Bear is a Great Chief."

Their anxiety for their survival faded and left them with the desire to take a large part in creating these lodges in their new land. Many would be needed as lodges must be built along with outbuildings and storage buildings for meat. These lodges must be strong enough to withstand hungry and large animals. Their Arapahoe brothers had much knowledge. The people were convinced that they would have lodges for their sleeping needs and living needs in a handful of sunrises.

Chief Storm Bear leapt quickly from his sleeping robes in order to greet Chief Black Kettle. They met at the mouth of the trail coming into Storm Bear's camp.

There were many Braves pulling horse-drawn travois carrying tools, hides, and much meat. Storm Bear could see their intentions. They were prepared to aid their adopted brothers; tears rose into his eyes. He was hugely grateful. He must express his feelings to Chief Black Kettle. Chief Storm Bear hallooed and waved his arms as they came close.

Black Kettle approached with the bearing of a Great Chief. He said, "Greetings, Storm Bear. We are here as promised. Are your people ready?"

Storm Bear said, "My people are ready and are more than willing to work. They only await your commands, Chief Black Kettle. My gratitude is immense. I give thanks to the Great Spirit for you and your Braves. You have saved us from a painful winter's death. Please see my heart and accept my feelings of devotion and truth."

The Medicine Man spoke, "He is sincere, dear Chief."

The Magic Man said, "His heart is big. He is near tears, Great Chief."

Chief Black Kettle nodded to Storm Bear, showing acceptance of his words. He said in a towering voice, "Braves, instruct Storm Bear's people. Let each proceed with their duties as their lifeblood allows. Love and respect Storm Bear's people. Listen to the old ones, there is still much to learn from them. Your gratefulness is appreciated, Storm Bear, but unnecessary. We are brothers. Lead the way, please."

THE CHOSEN ONES

Storm Bear's camp was in a state of comings and goings. Storm Bear and Black Kettle worked side by side with the Braves. Lodges rose quickly.

Hunters brought much game for the young women to butcher and to dry. Firewood piled up as far as the height of the new lodges. Horse barns were built to protect the horses from wild animals. The people were amazed and impressed to see the proficiency of Great Black Kettle's people.

Each of the adopted Arapahoe was assigned to the task they were physically able to perform. The oldest women sewed thick warm clothing. They learned from the old ones belonging to the Arapahoe how to waterproof these items. This knowledge would be passed down to the younger women during the cold and still winter months.

Storm Bear was proud; his people were learning the ways of the Arapahoe. He knew he would fail, but his courage would remain with him throughout his death. Even though, he vowed that his heart would not become bitter. His enormous heart could see that his people would survive. All knew that a Great Chief's duty is to protect and care for his people.

Arapahoe expertise brought with them a great respect to Storm Bear for the knowledge they shared freely. These astonishing people had made it possible for Storm Bear to do his duty by his people. The work was steady and lasted from sunrise up until moonrise during the expanse of fingers on Storm Bear's right hand.

Great Chief Black Kettle gazed about and said, "All is prepared. The adopted Arapahoe people will survive." He spoke to the Medicine and Magic Man, "Do you agree that all is done, my brothers?"

The Medicine spoke, "Oh Great Chief, I beg on Storm Bear's behalf that we make a gift of the tools belonging to the Arapahoe to Storm Bear's people. We have many tools in our possessions. Please, Great Chief, I can see that this is necessary for their survival."

Great Chief Black Kettle spoke, "I see that this is so, my caring Medicine Man. Yes, we will leave them with the tools."

The Magic Man spoke, "Great Chief, these tools will save Storm Bear's people, but they will not save Storm Bear. He is destined to perish during the end of this harsh winter coming upon us. We have no time to save him. The Great Spirit has let this be known to me. I will speak no more."

The Great Chief spoke, "I have also seen that he will not survive, my Magic Man. We must do what we can, but it will make no difference to Storm Bear. It is a pity, he is such a brave and humble Great Chief. However, he will fulfill his destiny. His name is written in the stars of the Spirit World. Through his efforts, he will save a remnant of his people. The Great Spirit loves his people. Storm Bear will be rewarded by the Great Spirit."

Chapter Fifty-Six

Storm Bear's anxieties decreased as he shivered from the cold winter wind. He watched the Great Chief Black Kettle lead his Arapahoe Braves back to their camp. He felt confident that the Colorado winter would be survived by his people with the aid his people had received from the Arapahoe. He felt that he had fulfilled his destiny. After all, had he not saved his people from certain death?

The old ones comprehended his lack of concern and discerned his pride in himself. They became uneasy. They knew Storm Bear had experienced little in the way of life. This they grasped from their own experiences. An earthly man can strive and then convince himself that he has taken all precautions against what will come. Yet, he fails. Life must be taken one day at a time. A man must also have the ability and the intelligence to adapt to life's ups and downs.

The old ones spoke to one another, "All know that youth is wasted on the young. We must be alert and help him when the challenges come. He is intelligent. He will become teachable. Shining Star has chosen wisely."

Shining Star watched from the Spirit World. As a Great Chief, he was aware that the Great Spirit required a man's whole heart and soul. Storm Bear had much to prove before he fulfilled his destiny. Shining Star knew Storm Bear was young, and it is the way of the young to be shortsighted. Storm Bear had to perceive this for himself. Shining Star also saw that Storm Bear would fulfill his destiny with his life. He reminded himself, he need only wait.

* * *

Winter came with a bone-chilling cold that brought with it a horrific blizzard. The people were confined to their lodges due to the blinding nature of the blizzard. They had never experienced such cold or so much snow. They did not know that they had yet to experience the length of winter in the Rockies. Winter comes early and will last more than a handspan of moons.

Suffering and sickness descended upon the people. They looked to Storm Bear to relieve them. Storm Bear commanded the Medicine Man and the Magic Man to see to the people's needs. He then begged the Great Spirit, "Please guide this inept Great Chief. I have been prideful. I have committed a great wrong. Your people need you, Great Spirit. I have not the knowledge to save them. Food supplies are dwindling, and the need for firewood has brought about the death of many of my good Braves who must search throughout these mountains. The children of my people are dying from the coughing sickness. It is as if an evil spirit has taken lodge in this camp." A vision flashed into his mind. The old ones were waiting. He said, "Thank you, Great Spirit. The old ones will help."

The old ones were waiting in a humble manner for Storm Bear to approach them. They were ancient. Even though, they still laid claim to much ingenuity. Storm Bear asked his Braves to bring the old ones safely to his lodge. They arrived with serious expressions. They had been watching and saw many dilemmas approaching the adopted Arapahoe tribe.

The Braves' numbers had been dwindling rapidly. This needed to be addressed immediately. The old ones spoke, "We must care for our Braves. They provide protection for our tribe, and they are strong. They must bind their selves together with hide strips from the buffalo when they leave the protection of the lodge to seek firewood and game. Let the women sew quickly so they may relieve their Braves of cold and wet clothing when they return. Without this precaution, they may become ill. We cannot cure them without the proper herbs. These herbs do not grow in cold weather."

At once, Storm Bear saw his mistake. The old ones would never berate a Great Chief for his lack of foresight. All knew herbs must be gathered, dried, and stored throughout the warm moons. He spoke, "I am responsible. I did not foresee illness among the tribe caused by these vicious storms. Oh, Great Spirit, did Shining Star make a terrible mistake by choosing me to be a Great Chief? I have failed. I did not see." His heart was overflowing with remorse. He could only hang his head in sorrow. Tears soon followed.

The old ones looked away and remained silent as Storm Bear wept. They did not show disrespect nor comfort to their Great Chief. Either could be misconstrued by a lesser man and bring him to despair. Despair was a very dangerous state of mind. It can lead to hopelessness and a lack of self-esteem. The old ones discerned that this chief's spirit would not be broken. He was not weak. His remorse made his heart fragile. He must learn, but he must not break. His mistakes did not make him unnecessary to this adopted Arapahoe tribe.

Storm Bear ceased weeping. He now realized that he had much to learn. He remembered that Shining Star had advised him to bring forth the old ones. Shining Star had also told him that he must rule without self-indulgence or fear. Storm Bear's heart transformed itself into a self-forgiving eagerness. The old ones had hoped and prayed to the Great Spirit. They now knew that Storm Bear would make the efforts required to save his people. These old ones rejoiced within their hearts. He had learned that all men walk the path the Great Spirit brings to them. This path is neither good nor bad. It is only necessary for the red man to survive the infiltration of the white man.

The red man believed that the white man had his own God. This God was cruel, bloodthirsty, and wished to do away with the red man. It did not occur to the red man that the white man did not hear their God. The Great Spirit did hear the people simply because of their belief and faith in him. He wished to preserve the red man. Storm Bear would be the last Great Chief with a destiny to fulfill. This was not known among the red man nor the white man.

The Great Spirit was with Storm Bear. This brought forth many ideas Storm Bear did not know he possessed. He was given the natural urge to be a Great Chief. The people's need for a Great Chief had not lessened. The Great Spirit had blessed them with the faith they needed to remain faithful to this Great Chief.

For the second time in his life, Storm Bear rose above his own emotional responses. He towered over the old ones. His black eyes were full of determination and displayed his resolve to be a Great Chief.

The old ones bowed and returned to their lodges to thank the Great Spirit. They knew it may be necessary to return to Storm Bear. However, too much knowledge given at once clouds the mind and does not touch the heart. Storm Bear's heart was clear and rich. It was for the best.

Storm Bear began by commanding the Medicine Man and the Magic Man to attend him for examining the lodges that stored meat, hides, food for the horses, and hides that provided clothing sewn by the women. He found all of these lodges were woefully supplied. He discovered that the food would not last through the winter. He made a decision to ration food stuff to all of the people, including himself and his holy men.

If attacked, they would need strong Braves; these ones must eat in a unit and would not be rationed. The horses were also necessary in an attack, but Storm Bear knew they may need to kill and butcher horses for food before the wild game returned in abundance to these mountains. When the blizzard ceased its shrieking and howling, he would send the Braves out on every clear sunrise to hunt and search for editable forest growth.

These plans brought the people hope. They would happily obey their Great Chief. Storm Bear had not thought it possible, but this blizzard would not end until several phases of the moon had passed.

Chapter Fifty-Seven

Before their adoption by the Arapahoe, the people were known as the Black Hills Tribe. They were a mild people and depended on trade and hunting for their meat. The harshness of this climate made them shiver and long for their home in the south. They had to leave their homes because they must flee the Warrior Women. These women were coming to slaughter these peaceful people and take their camp.

A Brave must not fight a woman. This law was passed from generation to generation among all red men. The Brave would not achieve the Spirit World if he should do such an unspeakable thing. The only exception to this law was in war. A Brave's woman will have his back in an attack from red and white men. Their women were well trained in this art. In any other circumstances, the women could not touch a weapon.

The Warrior Women had chosen not to live by this law. Their very name brought dread to the red and white alike. They were bent on death for all, especially the whites. The Black Hills Tribe could not bring themselves to disobey the Great Spirit. They set fire to their camp and left their peaceful life behind. They trusted their Great Chief, Shining Star, to lead them northwest. Shining Star completed his destiny. He saved his people, but for how long?

Storm Bear was challenged by the elements. It was a heavy responsibility for a man who was nearly a youth.

* * *

A twist of life is that things must get worse before they get better. Storm Bear was desperate. The stock of food was nearly gone. He thought, *Would I be known as the chief who starved his people unto their deaths?* He was frustrated. He felt as if he was going mad. His hands were tied.

The blizzard continued to howl outside of his lodge. The howling was almost more than he could bear. It became an enemy taunting him within his mind. There were so many things he could do for his people if he could just leave his lodge. His mind was blocked at every turn. He could do nothing but wait.

* * *

The Braves were keeping busy removing snow from the people's threshold and making paths to the horses' shelter. Lodges were nearly buried in snow. Firewood was in short supply.

THE CHOSEN ONES

The Braves had chopped trees, but the wood was green. This did not provide much heat, but it did produce much smoke. The people huddled around their firepits, trying to get warm while choking on smoke as it made its way to the smoke hole in the roof. They did not complain. It was just one more thing to endure.

Many of the red man's children died from the coughing sickness known as whooping cough by the whites.

The red man believed that their children no longer suffered. Death was a release. Their faith allowed for their elders to bring these children into the Spirit World. This brought much comfort to the red man.

The white man saw the loss of a child as a terrible punishment brought upon him. Grief dominated his thoughts. This stagnated the white man, sometimes for years.

The red man and the white man had always been worlds apart.

Storm Bear could not stop the blizzard; the people knew this well enough. Only the Great Spirit had the power to stop this killing blizzard. The people continued to pray for relief and for Storm Bear. Their faith was strong. They believed with heart and soul. They did not judge the Great Spirit when their prayers were not answered. They were sure that the Great Spirit did love his children and knew what was best. The old ones had seen this kind of killing storm in their youth. They knew the Great Spirit did not always intervene. Storm Bear had a destiny to fulfill. The Great Spirit would not help or hinder his chosen ones. They must make their own way to the Spirit World in spite of their difficulties. The old ones could not help. Storm Bear must prove his bravery and his courage. Shining Star could see the difficulties Storm Bear faced. He also knew the fate of the people was tied to the fate of the Great Chief. Many of the people would survive, and many would not. Storm Bear would learn that death is not to be feared and does not bring guilt to the living. Regardless, Shining Star had chosen wisely.

Chapter Fifty-Eight

Storm Bear woke to a quiet and bright morning, the first in many long moons. There was no time to waste. He and his Braves must hunt. He summoned them.

Storm Bear decided to walk uphill, following the river. He became more aware in the cold and crisp air. He hoped to find thirsty game breaking the thin ice patches. As he walked, he thought, *The river would be flowing soon.* He remembered playing in the river with the children when his tribe discovered Colorado. A large and happy smile crossed his worried and haggard face.

The snow was very deep, many handspans high. It had the feel of a squelching, melting snow. Storm Bear and his Braves saw that it was not cold. Their snow shoes were sinking into the snow. This was a warning to them, yet they did not understand. They continued to search for game. Suddenly, a huge deer leapt out of the underbrush. It did not scent the Braves; they were downwind from him. All the Braves fired their arrows. The buck dropped to the ground. The men were whooping and hollering at their achievement. They were playfully trying to determine which of them had made the killing shot.

Storm Bear smiled at their antics. He was pleased to see them happy again. The Braves were disturbed by a deep rumbling sound that shook the earth beneath their feet. They looked at one another and spoke joyfully, all of them at once, "The buffalo has returned!" They looked at the mountain peak, expecting to see a great herd of buffalo. Instead, they saw a wall of snow plummeting. The Braves tried to run from certain death, all except their Great Chief, Storm Bear. He met his death with bravery and courage.

Storm Bear remembered his last dream of suffocating blackness. He saw that the Great Spirit had prepared him for this death. He met it with another smile. He lost consciousness when he was buried under a huge mound of snow. His last thought was that winter was over and he had saved the people. Storm Bear had completed his destiny with bravery and courage.

Life is a great circle; it has no end. There are no Braves alive. Yet, the red man understood that all must die sometime. Every man must learn as he matures. All know the young are blind and that youth is wasted on the young.

The women and children have been left alone to care for themselves.

Even so, the Great Spirit would save a remnant of his people. These ones would bring descendants to right the wrongs done to the red man by the white man. Oh, there would be recommence of a sort. However, it would take many turns of the moon for these things to occur.

The Spirit World was watching and waiting for the justice due to the red man.

Milton Keynes UK
Ingram Content Group UK Ltd.
UKHW020440050324
438776UK00001BB/58